Ghost Stories
from the
American South

Ghost Stories from the American South

COMPILED AND EDITED BY W. K. McNEIL

August House / Little Rock

© 1985 by W.K. McNeil
Published 1985 by August House, Inc., P.O. Box 3223,
Little Rock, Arkansas, 72203, 501-663-7300

Printed in the United States of America

10 9 8 7 6

Library of Congress Cataloging-in-Publication Data

Main entry under title:

Ghost stories from the American South.

Includes index.
1. Ghosts—Southern States. I. McNeil, W. K.
BF1472.U6G48   1985   133.1'0975   84-45638
ISBN 0-935304-83-5
ISBN 0-935304-84-3 (pbk.)

Cover illustration and design by Byron Taylor
Line drawings by Jacqui Froelich
Design direction by Ted Parkhurst
Project direction by Liz Parkhurst

Texts 2, 10, 20, 29b and 58e are from the folklore archives of the
Regional Cultural Center, Arkansas College, Batesville, Arkansas, and
are reprinted with the permission of the college. Texts 19, 33, 47, 48,
49, 54, 59, 60, 64 and 80 originally appeared in North Carolina Folklore
and are reprinted with permission of the publisher.

To the memory of *Joe B. Rigdon*, a Southern mountaineer, who never had the opportunity for contact with books or scholarship. Knowing that a book was dedicated to him would have surprised him more than anyone else.

Contents

Acknowledgments

Compilers and authors of most books rely on the help of others for material necessary to make their proposed volume a reality. This tradition certainly holds for the present collection, for without outside help this manuscript would never have made it to the publisher's desk. A large number of people allowed me to intrude upon their busy lives and, in every case, responded graciously and kindly, willingly supplying me with the material found in this book. Such unselfishness deserves recognition, and I gladly give that here to Bill Clements, Bob Cochran, Frank de Caro, Nana Farris, Bill Ferris, George Foss, Bill Lightfoot, Brenda McCallum, Bob McCarl, Tom McGowan, Dan Patterson, Chuck Perdue, Sharon Sarthou, Ellen Shipley, Ethel C. Simpson, Marcia Wade, John O. West, and Charles K. Wolfe. They are, of course, not to be held responsible for any interpretations or errors found here; for those I claim sole responsibility.

W.K.M.

Introduction

This volume of supernatural narratives is, unlike most such volumes available today, taken from the folk tradition of the southern United States. A majority of the texts were collected in the last twenty-five years, although the tales are set in time periods ranging from the Revolutionary War to the present. Most of the items given here have never appeared in print before; in all cases, they have been maintained by oral narration. Some very widely known stories are given here, while others have not previously been known outside of a single family or community. They are related only in that they are in some sense Southern, meaning not that they are unique to the region but merely that they are told there.

These are examples of Southern folklore, primarily ghost legends, with some space given to closely related supernatural beings such as witches and banshees. I make no claim that all supernatural folk legends found in the South are set forth here or even that the ones to be found here are the most popular examples currently in existence. I have made a concerted attempt, however, to provide material representative of the entire Southern region.

Some items were taken from my own fieldwork, but most came from other collections and archives. Call it fate, accident, luck or chance; the point is that the informants whose texts fill these pages were not chosen by any design on my part. They just happened to have appropriate material which they could make readily available to me. Certainly, many other volumes of supernatural narratives could, provided informants could be ferreted out, be compiled, for almost every community and many families in the South have people who pass on these traditions.

A number of terms used in this volume may be unfamiliar or confusing to many readers. First is the word *folklore*, which in popular usage is generally reserved for anything that is quaint or odd. That is not the precise meaning of the word, however, and not the one used in this book. Here, *folklore* refers to material that is passed on orally and, usually, informally; is traditional; undergoes change over space and time, creating variants and versions; is usually anonymous in the sense that most bearers of folklore are not concerned with the original creator; and finally, folklore is usually formulaic.[1]

Another term which calls for definition is *legend*. Legends are one of three types of folk narratives, the other two being folktales and myths. Folktales are regarded as fictional by both teller and audience and are told primarily for entertainment. Myths are set in prehistoric times, involve the activities of gods, demigods and animals and are believed by the teller to be true. Legends are set in historic times, are concerned with secular characters and call for a position of belief or disbelief.

Equally confusing is the common word *ghost*. Its ambiguity results because many terms—ghost, revenant, wraith, specter, apparition and spirit, to name a few—are used for essentially the same phenomenon. Often the actions of these agents are indistinguishable from those of witches. Ernest W. Baughman comments on the difficulty of distinguishing between these various figures:

> It is very difficult to tell whether the haunters under this category are ghosts, witches, or familiar spirits. The actions of these agents are very much alike. About the only distinction that can be made is that made by the informant: if the informant thinks of the agent as a ghost, then the agent is a ghost, regardless of the similarities of the actions to those of witches or spirits. The famous "Bell Witch" of Tennessee is usually a ghost by any criteria used; yet it is almost invariably referred to as a witch.[2]

Complicating the matter of definition is that the returning dead come back in several forms. First, they may come back in the same body they had while alive; second, they may appear in some sort of spectral form; third, they may be invisible and known only by the deeds, noises or mischief they commit.

In this book, for the sake of simplicity, a *ghost* is defined as a being returned from the dead in human or animal form or having some features of humans or animals. Those returning dead which lack human or animal features are labeled *supernatural creatures*. *Witches* differ from ghosts mainly in that they are living people with supernatural powers rather than dead people who have returned. The *banshee* mentioned earlier is regarded as a ghost although placed in a chapter dealing with non-ghosts. In a treatise on Irish or Scottish folklore, a banshee would likely be classified as a *fairy*, but these small, delicate supernatural creatures are extremely rare in American folklore.

One further definition is in order, namely "the South." That is easily answered, for it refers to the states of Alabama, Arkansas, Florida, Georgia, Kentucky, Louisiana, Mississippi, North Carolina, South Carolina, Tennessee, Texas and Virginia. In other words, the South means here most of the states represented in the Confederacy during the Civil War.

Having established some working definitions, it remains for me to discuss those who preserve and propagate these legends, that is, the informants. Remarks about individual narrators are included in the section of notes in the back of the book, but some general consideration should be given to the type of person who communicates legends about the supernatural.

The stereotype exists that the best bearers of any sort of folk tradition, ghost legends included, are rustic illiterates. As with most stereotypes, this has an element of truth but is also misleading. Certainly the rural unschooled know and tell such stories, but by no means do they have an exclusive hold on them. Ghost narratives flourish in cities just as well as they do in bucolic areas; indeed, they may even be more common there simply because there are more people to hear and tell them. Suffice it to say that most Southerners—in fact, most Americans—know or know of such tales, which they have heard related by friends and acquaintances, sometimes as firsthand experiences but more often as something that happened to a friend of a friend.

What type of person tells ghost stories? The foremost qualification for a bearer of this or any type of folklore is intelligence; a second requirement is a good memory. Without these, he will not be able to recall the lore and certainly will not be able to supply the details that remove a text from the status of a mundane incident to that of an item of interest that others want to hear.

Notice that I mentioned intelligence, not education, for the two are not synonymous. A person with no formal schooling may still be quite intelligent; furthermore, education has little if any bearing on whether or not a person will relate any type of folklore. As the texts in this volume illustrate, many ghost legends are perpetuated by college students, while others come from people with minimal schooling. To put it briefly, almost any intelligent person with a good memory who has the interest can, and will, tell stories concerning ghosts and other supernatural creatures.

Though there are many people who fit that description, certain narrators are better than others. To distinguish between these good narrators and those who can tell a tale but don't, Swedish folklorist Carl Wilhelm von Sydow offered the concept of active and passive bearers of tradition. He defined active bearers as those "who keep tradition alive and transmit it, whereas the passive bearers have indeed heard of what a certain tradition contains, and may perhaps, when questioned, recollect part of it, but do nothing themselves to spread it or keep it alive."[3]

One mark of the active bearer is that he tells a story as though it is his own, not necessarily as a personal experience (although it may be), but one that is related with authority as if it is his possession. The active narrator has thorough command of a text and presents it strongly. He will flesh out the basic narrative with dialogue and various dramatic devices so that it becomes a performance, not just a skeletal presentation of the merely essential details.

The passive bearer, on the other hand, presents his material almost apologetically and relates it as a secondhand possession, frequently resorting to phrases like "they say" or "it is said," not for clarification but because he is ill at ease with it.

Perhaps the difference between an active bearer and a passive bearer's treatments of a ghost legend is best illustrated by concrete examples. First, a text from Tavares, Florida:

> Four or five years ago the exciting thing to do on a Friday or Saturday evening was go to Monkey Jungle. Monkey Jungle was a long winding road with many overhanging trees. The road eventually wound up where it began, thus creating a large circle.
> It was believed that on a full moon after you crossed eight railroad tracks and stopped on the ninth, you would see a black body carrying her head. It was told her son had been hit by a train. So the next night she laid her head on the tracks for a train to run over.[4]

Second, a text from Harrisonburg, Virginia:

> There is a haunted house in Mt. Sidney. The first owner was a lady who went crazy. Since then there have been several owners who say the house is haunted because at night they hear footsteps, and the blinds are open in the morning that they drew the night before.[5]

Third, a narrative from Jonesboro, Arkansas:

> There was an old cemetery down the road from their farm. Uh, uh, of course, they called it a graveyard. Their, uh, grandparents had always told them that this old grave there was the

grave of a drunkard. The legend was that once when he was drunk and eating cherries, he choked to death on a cherry pit. And then, of course, this tremendous cherry tree grew at the spot where his head would be in the grave. It was quite old and had low, spreading branches. All the children who lived around were just frightened to death of it because of the legend. And, uh, that's just about all I can think of except that, you know, one summer evening, late, at twilight time, Big Mother was riding a horse down the road when in some manner the horse wandered off into the graveyard. You know, when she found out where she was, she became frightened and that frightened her horse and he began to run. He crossed the grave and the low hanging branches dragged her off the horse. That's just all I know, I don't know how she got home or anything.[6]

These three narrators clearly have an uninvolved, almost disinterested, manner of presentation. They all recall the basic details of the legends they are relating, but they make no attempt to heighten the dramatic effect of the stories and, in the case of the third text, there is some hesitancy even in remembering the details recalled. Reading a transcript of their renditions is like scanning an outline rather than the complete play. Compare them with the following three texts. First, one from Forrest City, Arkansas:

The bank was robbed by a man who held the bank up by himself with a shotgun. He was apprehended a short time later but didn't have the money with him. A policeman panicked and shot the man on sight before the man had a chance to tell anyone where he hid the money. As the man was dying, they asked him where he hid the money, and he said he hid it in the old graveyard south of town behind the huge oak tree.

The police immediately go there to look for the money, but they never find it. They assumed that the man lied and that the town lost the ten thousand dollars. Then some teenage boys decide to investigate and they find a couple of dollars buried under the tree. The cops investigate again and find nothing. Time after time only a few dollars at a time was found under the tree; but when it's investigated by police nothing has been found by their digging. Everyone believes that the money is somewhere under the tree, but they believe the man put a curse on the money. Everyone believes that the curse will go away some day so they keep trying to find the money.[7]

Second, another narrative from Arkansas, this one from Batesville:

> There was this woman who hated her husband. So one night she murdered him and cut him up into thirteen pieces. About a week later she was lying in bed when she heard a voice calling, "Where are my legs?" She just put her pillow over her head and soon the voice stopped. The next night she heard the same voice asking, "Where are my arms?" and the next night the voice asked, "Where are my hands?" She finally got a little afraid and went to stay at a neighbor's house for a night. Nothing happened there so she went home again the next night. That night she heard the voice again wailing, "Where is my left thumb?" over and over and over. Suddenly her left thumb began to twitch and it was twisted off.[8]

Finally, there is this text from Hot Springs, Arkansas:

> Mrs. Florencie Williams lived in a large house on Grand Avenue. Her son, Bob Williams, had been sheriff and was shot to death. Thus, Mrs. Williams lived with Mrs. Woodcock only.
> Mrs. Woodcock was a friend of my grandmother Henderson. She told Granny that many times when she came into the house, at night after 10:30, at the top of the stairs there were three figures. When she reached the top of the stairs the figures would disappear into the walls. There was one certain door upstairs which would not stay closed. No matter how many times Mrs. Woodcock would close it, it would *click* and open.
> At a place in the upstairs hall was a big mirror. At certain times of the year there would appear on the mirror a ghostly looking thing as if someone had soaped the mirror for a Halloween prank. Mrs. Woodcock would rub it off and it wouldn't appear until the next year.
> Mrs. Woodcock told Granny that often she would walk up the stairs and she would hear a *click, click* noise following her up. When she stopped, it stopped. It sounded like a child playing in high heels or shoes with copper taps on the heels.
> Mrs. Florencie never had any flowers in the house—at least she never went out to buy any and didn't have a garden. But sometimes in the dead of winter, when there weren't any fresh flowers for miles around, they would smell tube roses. The smell would start out faint and then increase to a terribly strong smell.

Every so often, every picture in the house would be found turned at an angle clockwise. Mrs. Woodcock and Mrs. Florencie would straighten them up and later would find them crooked again.[9]

In the last three texts an altogether different tale-telling ability is evident. The narrator is in total command of the narrative; there is nothing lackadaisical or hesitant about the presentations. None is offered as a personal experience, but all of the stories in a sense belong to the person telling it. That state of authority is almost totally lacking in the three earlier yarns.

A not uncommon situation is for passive and active bearers to change their relationship to folk tradition. Passive bearers might become active if they hear a tradition long enough that they become conversant with it and take it actively in hand. On the other hand, active bearers may become passive for various reasons. For example, a child may know actively several items of children's folklore but become passive concerning them once he has outgrown his childhood. An active bearer may also become passive when there is no longer an audience for the traditions he knows. But with legendary material such as is presented in this volume, most active and passive narrators remain so all of their lives.

Granted that there are both active and passive narrators, where do they narrate? What is the ambiance in which ghost legends are narrated? The answer is simple: they are told in most places where more than one person can be found. The performer/audience distance is usually not so great as that between a concert pianist and those attending his recital, but one thing is certain: without an audience, the narrator will cease to narrate.

In times past, the home was a place where ghost and supernatural legends were told, and it remains an important arena for the transmission of such material. Often ghost stories are told just between members of the immediate family, but on other occasions, a special social gathering, such as a party for friends, elicits such activity. In the South, country stores are an important forum for the exchange of tales, although usually in these situations the transmission is between members of the same generation rather than from an older generation to a younger one. The same holds for another popular place where ghost legends are told: the college dormitory. A typical dorm session is described by a female student:

On November 23, 1974 it was very rainy and dark. Around

9:00 I went to Room 627 to visit. The wind was hollering through the cracked window. One of the girls put a a candle in the middle of the room, and turned out the lights.[10]

Campfires, offices and automobiles, during long trips, could also be cited as places where ghost stories are commonly related.

Why do people tell ghost stories? There is no single answer to this question, because most tales are told for more than one reason. The late William R. Bascom divided the various functions of folklore into four basic types: *compensation, validation, education* and *integration*. These terms sound good, but what do they mean? Again, perhaps the best way to demonstrate is by example. For the first function, that of *compensation,* consider the following story:

Children heard of a piano playing in a church outside of Osceola, about four miles out of town. They were curious and set out to satisfy their curiosity. They said they actually heard the piano playing but they were afraid to go inside of the church to verify the noise they heard. They left immediately in a hurry to get back to Osceola. The driver of the car was going very fast on loose rocks, a gravel road, and lost control of the car and hit an embankment. Two was dead on arrival at the Osceola hospital and three escaped with minor injuries.[11]

The collector of this narrative made the following assessment: "I believe that this legend served to compensate for the accident. There was an accident and two people were killed. So, to compensate for the man's inadequacies [losing control of the car], there is the implied belief that the supernatural connected with the playing piano caused the accident." Undoubtedly, this tale serves several other functions, but it is plain that its main purpose is that which the collector has underscored.

Validation, the second of the four functions in Bascom's scheme, involves justifying cultural rituals and institutions. For example, a woman related the following narrative, which she said contains a message warning everyone to "live a Christian life, because you never know when you will die."

About forty years ago when I was twenty, my boyfriend and I were double-dating with my best friend and her fiancé. We were going to a wedding party that Saturday night that was being given in honor of my girlfriend, who was going to be married the following Saturday. The party was similar to wedding showers today in the gift-giving custom only. The showers then were more of a party in nature and your fiancé, boyfriend or husband were invited also.

After the presents were opened, a party began in full bloom. There was a tremendous amount of food enjoyed, then music and dancing began. We had all been having a good time for about two hours when I developed a migraine headache. My headache continually worsened until I couldn't stand it for another minute. I had to go home. My boyfriend and I caught a ride with another couple that was leaving because we had rode in my girlfriend's fiancé's car, and of course, since they were the honored couple, they weren't read to leave yet.

I got home around eleven o'clock and I went straight to bed. At one o'clock my mother awakened me with a horrible phone call. My girlfriend had been instantly killed in an automobile accident on the way home from the party. Her fiancé hadn't been seriously injured. The accident occurred when they were topping a hill and a car with a drunk man driving hit them head on. The girl was only nineteen, and everyone was shocked and grieved that someone so sweet, young and beautiful could have been killed so horribly. Those that were close to her were hurt the most, including me and her family, of course.

After she was buried in the Catholic cemetery, her parents bought her a beautiful tombstone in the shape of an angel. Legend has it that every time someone visits her grave, the angel tombstone points her finger at them and the pointed finger follows them around the graveyard until they leave. It's been said that the finger lights up at night with a golden glow. I have seen the finger point at me when I visited the grave. It's as if the statue has suddenly come to life as it points at you while you're walking. I believe you can see these things because my girlfriend was such a virtuous girl and the angel tombstone was an appropriate memorial of the innocent young girl who had lived a Christian life.[12]

What the legend really means is, of course, a matter of speculation. Some persons might say that it contains an anti-religious message. According to others familiar with the story, the girl's parents "were possessed with their religion, and they believed practically everything was a sin"[13]; these observers might argue that the legend contains a lesson for parents who are very strict. To the informant, however, the main function the narrative served was validation of the Christian outlook on life.

That folklore often functions as a form of *education* should be obvious to most readers. Many people are familiar with fables or folktales that point out some moral. In some societies, formal instructions are given in various forms of folklore. That is not often the case in the United States; more frequently, legends are used to make such points as that enunciated by this informant, who said a ghost appeared to remind people of the evil of unjust execution:

> Forty years ago a man was hung on the bridge in Forrest City across from the courthouse. He was hung because he killed a man in self-defense, but the police said that he killed the man purposely. A friend of mine knew the man, and he said that they were at a bar drinking when the man and a stranger got into an argument. The stranger pulled out a gun. The man grabbed the gun, and after a struggle the gun went off and shot the stranger. My friend saw what happened, and he said he knew it was self-defense. After a short unjust trial, the man was pronounced guilty, and he was hung the following day.
>
> I heard for many years that you could see the man hanging from the bridge on the anniversary of his death. I didn't believe it for years until a friend invited me to go with him and see the man hanging there, about fifteen years ago, on the anniversary of his death. A light flashed where he had been hung and you could actually see a vision of a man hanging for about three minutes, and then it was gone.[14]

Folklore also is used to maintain conformity to accepted patterns of behavior, or *integration*. While this is partially achieved through the previously mentioned functions of education and validation, Bascom's concept of integration differs in that it can refer to situations in which folklore is used to exert social pressure. It can also refer to situations in which oral traditions are used against individuals who attempt to deviate from patterns of convention. Most instances of folklore used to achieve integration are not so extreme; usually it does little more than bind those who know an item of lore into a group. This is precisely the integrative function that the following legend serves:

> About a mile from the rural town of Chapel Hill, Tennessee, a railroad track crosses a gravel road. In the 1890s an engineer

for the Louisville & Nashville Railroad was killed here. This man got too close to the edge of the cab, and as they sped around a sharp curve he fell from the train. He was decapitated as the train rolled on.

Every night at 9:30, the L&N freight train passes this area. Shortly afterwards, a light appears which sways back and forth. This is supposedly the headless engineer searching for his head.[15]

Because the present book is devoted to orally transmitted ghost legends, which differ from the literary stories most readers are familiar with, a few words about the two types of narratives are in order. Of course, oral and literary legends are alike in some respects, such as the tendency to concentrate on a leading character, but the differences are greater. One of the major distinctions is that folk legends usually have no title. Typically, the traditional ghost tale begins with some statement like, "You recall old Arnold Hill? Well, did you hear that story about him and the sailor's ghost?" And if these tales have a title at all, it is of only the most general, descriptive sort.

A second feature of folk legends is that they generally consist of only one scene. Compare, for example, the following tale with a more complex literary legend:

John Green and Jim Cook were walking to church one night back in 1905 or 1906. They were going to Cook's Chapel down near Savoy. As they walked along they saw a group of men up in front. The boys decided to catch them and walk together. The faster Jim and John walked, the faster the men walked and the taller they grew until they were as tall as the trees. The men came to a big rock by the side of the road; here a hollow led off into the woods. When the men came to this rock, they turned off behind it and disappeared. When the boys got to the spot, they could see no one. Later, Jim and John went back there and looked over the whole area during daylight but they could find nothing unusual. They always believed this vision had a meaning for them but they never knew what.[16]

Unlike literary legends, which are the work of the writer, folk legends are not composed by the presenter; he is merely the means by which the story is passed on and perpetuated. Even in the case of narratives based on personal experiences, the audience is, in certain respects, more important than the narrator, for without them the legends cease to be told. On the other hand, composers of literary legends write in hopes of capturing an audience and produce material that may, or may not, be successful. Thus, William Austin wrote "Peter Rugg, the Missing Man," which was so successful that it passed into local legendry.

Another notable difference between oral and literary legends is that the former lacks constant form; instead, it is in a continual state of flux. Even when repeated by the same narrator, two tellings of a story are never identical. Oral legends are generally related in vernacular language, because that is the way most people ordinarily speak. Regarding his narrative as something that actually happened, or is said to have happened (as is not the case in literary legends, especially literary ghost legends), the teller of folk legends relates his text in the language his audience will understand, that is, his daily speech. Certainly some literary texts are couched in vernacular language; mostly, however, the literary tradition attempts to avoid the colloquial.

There is also an added physical dimension to the orally transmitted ghost legend which often makes it difficult to capture in print: the narrator's use of his voice and body to dramatize the text. Facial expressions, manual gestures, and vocal intonation and inflection are utilized to bring a story to life. Factors of time and space also condition the performance, and, of course, the audience has a more direct impact upon the text than is the case with a written piece. Certainly, then, the oral ghost narrative differs markedly from the literary one.

Others have preceded the current volume with collections and analyses of Southern ghostlore, but there haven't been as many as one might think, especially when one discounts nonscholarly efforts. One of the most successful early efforts was made by Charles M. Skinner, a one-time newspaper correspondent who produced five volumes of American legendry between 1896 and 1903. The first of these, a two-volume *Myths and Legends of Our Own Land* (1896), was followed by *Myths and Legends of Our New Possessions and Protectorate* (1899), which was followed in turn by the two-volume *American Myths and Legends* (1903).

As these titles indicate, Skinner's focus was on legends of all sorts found in the United States and her possessions rather than on supernatural legends from the South. Most of the space is given to items from the Middle Atlantic and New England States, but even so, a goodly portion of the 1896 and 1903 volumes deal with the South and some of those texts deal with the supernatural. All of the selections were "improved" by Skinner, who related the tales in what Richard Dorson calls a "limpid Hawthornesque prose."[17] Although frankly a popularizer, Skinner did collect material from oral tradition and made some attempt to provide his books with some scholarly trappings, such as prefaces demonstrating how the legends fitted into regional clusters. Nevertheless, he also took items from various printed sources that often remain unidentified. Most of his texts deal with Colonial and Revolutionary times; he deliberately stayed with eras beyond the memory of the living mean, because "the past is more picturesque than the present."[18] Rewritten texts, the failure to identify sources, and the lack of comparative material place Skinner's volume outside the realm of ideal folklore scholarship.

Newbell Niles Puckett's *Folk Beliefs of the Southern Negro* (1926) was originally written as a Ph.D. dissertation at Yale University. It does include one chapter dealing with ghosts and witches, although it consists mainly of descriptions of beliefs about these beings rather than complete texts. Puckett's book is a study of acculturation and, despite a title that implies otherwise, consists of materials gathered from elderly people and rural illiterates. He also associated folklore with the past, a misleading concept to which many other scholars have subscribed. Thus, he spoke about "the necessity of haste in collecting this fast-disappearing lore."[19]

Although Frank Clyde Brown began collecting his folklore prior to Puckett, his work was not published until long afterwards. Indeed, it did not find its way into print until after Brown's death when it appeared as the seven-volume *Frank C. Brown Collection of North Carolina Folklore* (1952–1964). Brown had come to Trinity College (now Duke University) in 1909 as a Professor of English, and three years later started gathering various types of folklore found in the Tarheel State.

Brown's interest lay mainly in folksongs and ballads, but he did collect several folktales and legends, a large number of which deal with ghosts and the supernatural. Brown did record his informants' names and usually their place of residence and the site of the collection. In recording these, he did not consider such factors as degree of belief or nonbelief; contextual data; or what role the narrative had in the community in which it was kept alive. There is also ample evidence that much of what he recorded was "memory culture," that is, material recalled from the past but no longer actively told. Brown's total work is useful, if for no other reason, because it is one of the most extensive collections from a single state ever published. In regard to ghost legends, however, it is a relatively small body of work.

One of the most prolific American collectors of the genres of folklores sometimes collectively called the verbal arts (meaning those items like songs or stories that are regarded by their perpetuators as requiring artistic performance) was Vance Randolph. A native of Pittsburg, Kansas, he spent most of his adult life in the Ozarks of Arkansas, Missouri and Oklahoma. Among his numerous publications were articles on witchcraft; a booklet titled *Ozark Ghost Stories* (1944); and a book originally issued as *Ozark Superstitions* (1947).[20]

This last volume is especially valuable because of its bibliography listing everything written on traditional Ozark beliefs as of the publication date. Two lengthy chapters deal with Ozark ghost stories and witchcraft. The stories are generally rewritten summaries, but a few are offered in the actual words of his informants, who are identified by name and place of residence.

J. Mason Brewer was one of the leading black folklorists of his day. Throughout his long career, he taught in colleges in North and South Carolina and Texas. Like the other scholars mentioned here, he was interested in many types of folk narrative found in the South, and several of his books do include some ghost tales. His *Dog Ghosts and Other Texas Negro Folk Tales* (1958) is seemingly devoted to the subject; the title, however, is misleading. Only the last of the book's five sections deals with ghost stories. Brewer includes informant names, ages at the time of collection and places of residence. He also tries to reproduce his texts exactly as they were related to him; for the convenience of his readers, however, he regularizes the dialect, which lessens the value of including dialect spelling. Another shortcoming in the collection is that Brewer, like too many other collectors, offers no comparative material.[21]

(On the positive side, Brewer avoids one trap that many collectors often fall into, namely, the geriatric syndrome. Rather than recording only from elderly informants, he garners legends from many age groups. His informants range in age from twenty-one to ninety-seven.)

Two collectors of Kentucky mountain lore did include comparative data, but their work had other problems. Marie Campbell's *Tales from the Cloud Walking Country* (1958) was devoted to tales "from across the ocean waters" that were grouped around individual raconteurs.[22] The texts were mostly märchen, or fairy tales, with only a few ghost narratives included. Recent evidence suggests that some of these tales were fabricated out of whole cloth. Whether or not this is so, it is clear that the material Campbell reported was representative of a "memory culture" rather than a living one.

To a certain extent, this is also true of the work of Leonard Roberts, who definitely sought out the oldest elements of folklore but did manage to report some more recent items. His focus was on märchen, but in *South from Hell-fer-Sartin* (1955) and *Sang Branch Settlers: Folksongs and Tales of a Kentucky Mountain Family* (1974), a few selections deal with ghost and supernatural legends.

Ray B. Browne's *"A Night With the Hants" and Other Alabama Folk Experiences* (1977) not only includes comparative data and notes on informants but a transcript of a folk storytelling session. By this means, Browne provides as close a flavor of the natural context as one is likely to find. Despite the title, there is much in Browne's book that does not have anything to do with ghosts or the supernatural. Still, the majority does. Although Browne has no apparent age bias in his collecting, most of his texts come from persons of advanced age. Despite his claim that the volume "represents a good cross section of the folktales of the state," the truth is that only a very small section of Alabama is represented.[23] Even so, it is the only collection of printed ghost legends from the state and gives more information about the setting in which such narratives are often related than any other book yet published.

One of the most prolific authors among American folklorists was the late Richard M. Dorson. Of his more than two dozen books and hundreds of articles, only two deal with Southern ghost lore, and even in these the subject receives scant attention. A few brief items, such as John Lawson's report of a spectral ship that appeared to colonists of present-day North Carolina, are included in *America Begins: Early American Writing* (1950).[24] Several supernatural texts are contained in *American Negro Folktales* (1967), itself a compilation of two earlier books, *Negro Folktales in Michigan* (1956) and *Negro Tales from Pine Bluff, Arkansas, and Calvin, Michigan* (1958).[25] Dorson includes informant and collection data, as well as comparative notes, but the volume's major value lies in the extended introductory essay containing, among other features, a discussion of the "Art of Negro Storytelling."[26]

Two other works which deal tangentially with ghost narratives are John A. Burrison's *The Golden Arm: The Folk Tale and Its Literary Use by Mark Twain and Joel C. Harris* (1968) and Harry Middleton Hyatt's *Hoodoo, Conjuration, Witchcraft, Rootwork* (1970–1977). Burrison's monograph concerns a tale that is always told as fiction but is based on an ancient folk belief that a dead man or animal cannot rest until its physical remains are intact. Hyatt's several volumes contain data gathered during many years of collecting, primarily among blacks, which focus on the four aspects of belief listed in the title. The first volume contains several texts concerning ghosts as well as informants' statements about the stories.[27]

William Lynwood Montell's *Ghosts Along the Cumberland: Deathlore in the Kentucky Foothills* (1975) is the most recent scholarly treatment of Southern ghostlore. As the subtitle suggests, Montell deals with more than ghosts, namely, death beliefs, death omens and folk beliefs. The major importance of this volume is that it deals with material from a very small region, an area of southcentral Kentucky known as the Eastern Pennyroyal. Surprisingly, there are very few other studies of ghostlore, or any other type of folklore, from such essentially homogenous sections of the South. Filled with comparative data, information on collectors and informants and discussions of various aspects of deathlore, *Ghosts Along the Cumberland* reveals just how strong a hold tradition exerts on daily life in the South.[28]

That, to my knowledge, constitutes the entire body of published books on Southern ghost legendry. Such popularizing efforts as Hans Holzer's *Best True Ghost Stories* (1983) were not mentioned because of both their nonscholarly design and their nonfolkloristic approach. Holzer and similar pop-parapsychologists are primarily concerned with demonstrating that ghosts exist and are "indicative of man's continued existence beyond death."[29]

This is not the aim of folklorists, who are interested in ghost narratives as an element of traditional culture. Whether or not ghosts exist, they are psychologically real. People do believe in them and tell stories about them, which makes them deserving of consideration and study. Questions that concern folklorists are, Who sees and talks about ghosts? Under what conditions? What do they mean as cultural artifacts? Hopefully, some answers to these queries are given in this book in the prefatory comments to each section and the notes for each entry.

Now it only remains to discuss one of the eight categories this book contains. Why does a volume of ghost stories have a section on witches? There are at least two reasons. One is the desire on my part to provide some examples of other types of closely related supernatural lore, especially since these traditions are often perpetuated by the same people who tell ghost stories. More important is the already mentioned fact that in societies such as the South where both witches and ghosts exist, there is no sharp distinction between them.

So much for the preliminaries. Now on to some stories of the eerie and supernatural that are told in the South.

W.K. McNeil

Ozark Folk Center
Mountain View, Arkansas

Notes

[1]For a more detailed discussion of these points, see my book *The Charm Is Broken: Readings in Arkansas and Missouri Folklore* (Little Rock: August House, Inc., 1984), pp. 11–13.

[2]Ernest W. Baughman, *Type and Motif Index of the Folktales of England and North America* (The Hague: Mouton & Co., 1966), p. 143.

[3]Carl Wilhelm von Sydow, *Selected Papers on Folklore* (New York: Arno Press, 1977; reissue of a work originally published in 1948), pp. 12–13.

[4]Reported in 1978 by Terry Fox from Tavares, Florida. Fox was apparently recalling a legend that was popular during his teenage years. This is Baughman's motif E422.1.1(b) "Headless woman—appearance only."

[5]Collected September, 1965 by Elmer L. Smith from an unidentified informant in Harrisonburg, Virginia. Baughman's motifs E281 "Ghosts haunt house" and E402.1.2 "Footsteps of invisible ghost heard" apply here.

[6]Collected June 15, 1974 by Katherine McCracken from an unnamed white female in Jonesboro, Arkansas. There is no motif number cited by either Baughman or Thompson that directly corresponds to the element of the cherry tree in this text.

[7]Collected by Brenda Hedrick from an unnamed retired contractor in Forrest City, Arkansas. The man had lived in Forrest City for the past fifty-five years; the bank was robbed about thirty-five years before. He claimed he saw some of the money that was found and strongly believed that the money was cursed by the robber. Baughman's motif E291 "Ghosts protect hidden treasure" is relevant.

[8]Collected in 1975 by Lynn Runyan from an unidentified informant in Batesville, Arkansas. This is very reminiscent of Type 366 *The Man from the Gallows* and Baughman's motifs E235.4 "Return from the dead to punish theft of part of corpse" and E419.7 "Ghost returns when part of body is removed from grave." Runyan's text differs from most in that the corpse is mutilated without being buried and the ending lacks the sudden scare tactic of hollering at a listener "You've got it!" or some similar phrase, and it does not have the unrealistic silver or gold arm, which is of course the reason this tale is often called "The Golden Arm."

[9]Collected by Ruthann Luedicke in 1961 from her aunt, Ruth Henderson Martin. The informant was a native of Marshall, Texas, but at the time of this collection lived in Hot Springs, Arkansas. Martin also contributed the text about the dead soldier at Pleasant Hill, Louisiana, who returned for his missing teeth (21 in text), and more information about her is given in the notes for that narrative. Relevant motifs here include E281 "Ghosts haunt house" and E402.1.2 "Footsteps of invisible ghost heard." There is no assigned motif number for the ghostly flowers; the closest is F815 "Extraordinary plants."

[10]These comments appear in a paper turned in to Dr. William Clements, Arkansas State University, Jonesboro, Arkansas, by Katherine Lemay.

[11]Collected June 16, 1974, in Jonesboro, Arkansas, by Artie Faye Taylor from Mrs. Annie Jackson, a twenty-five year old black woman. The informant was a language arts teacher in elementary schools in Osceola, Arkansas. The relevant motif is E402.1.3 "Invisible ghost plays musical instrument."

[12]Collected in 1974 by Brenda Hedrick from an unnamed sixty-year-old woman.

The woman is a devout Catholic, and according to Hedrick, "her religion is so intense that she has never missed going to church unless she was extremely sick." The relevant motif is F990 "Inanimate object acts as if living."

[13]Collected in 1974 by Brenda Hedrick from an unnamed retired electrician in Forrest City, Arkansas. The man was sixty years old and a lifelong resident of Forrest City.

[14]Collected in 1974 by Brenda Hedrick in Forrest City, Arkansas, from an unnamed retired farmer who lived near the town. The relevant motif is E274(a) "Ghost haunts scene of unjust execution."

[15]Collected in 1978 by Carl May from an unidentified informant. The relevant motifs are E422.1.1 "Headless revenant" and E530.1 "Ghost-like lights."

[16]Collected July 1, 1981, by Beulah Faye Tucker Davis from Belle Davis Green in Fayetteville, Arkansas. There is no motif number listed that exactly fits the incident described in Green's story; the closest is the general motif D600 "Miscellaneous transformation incidents."

[17]Richard M. Dorson, "How Shall We Rewrite Charles M. Skinner Today?," in Wayland D. Hand, ed., *American Folk Legend: A Symposium* (Berkeley: University of California Press, 1971), p. 69.

[18]Charles M. Skinner, *Myths and Legends of Our Own Land*, 2 vols. (Philadelphia: J.B. Lippincott, 1896), vol. I, p. 257.

[19]Newbell Niles Puckett, *Folk Beliefs of the Southern Negro* (Chapel Hill, North Carolina: University of North Carolina Press, 1926), p. viii.

[20]The book was reissued in 1964 by Dover Publications, Inc. as *Ozark Magic and Folklore*. Despite the title change, there were no alterations in the book's contents.

[21]J. Mason Brewer, *Dog Ghosts and Other Texas Negro Folk Tales* (Austin, Texas: University of Texas Press, 1958).

[22]Marie Campbell, *Tales from the Cloud Walking Country* (Bloomington, Indiana: Indiana University Press, 1958), p. 9.

[23]Ray B. Browne, *"A Night with the Hants" and Other Alabama Folk Experiences* (Bowling Green, Ohio: Bowling Green University Popular Press, 1977), p. xx.

[24]Richard M. Dorson, *America Begins: Early American Writing* (Bloomington, Indiana: Indiana University Press, 1971; reissue of a work originally published in 1950). Lawson's account appears on p. 159, and other supernatural incidents involving a Southern setting are on pp. 151 and 156.

[25]Richard M. Dorson, *Negro Folktales in Michigan* (Cambridge, Massachusetts: Harvard University Press, 1956) and Richard M. Dorson, *Negro Tales from Pine Bluff, Arkansas and Calvin, Michigan* (Bloomington, Indiana: Indiana University Press, 1958).

[26]Richard M. Dorson, *American Negro Folktales* (Greenwich, Connecticut: Fawsett Publications, Inc., 1967). "The Art of Negro Storytelling" appears on pp. 47–59.

[27]Harry Middleton Hyatt, *Hoodoo, Conjuration, Witchcraft, Rootwork* (New York: Alma Egan Hyatt Foundation, 1970), vol. I, pp. 19–56.

[28]William Lynwood Montell, *Ghosts Along the Cumberland: Deathlore in the Kentucky Foothills* (Knoxville: University of Tennessee Press, 1975).

[29]Hans Holzer, *Best True Ghost Stories* (Englewood Cliffs, New Jersey: Prentice-Hall, Inc., 1983), p. 5.

1 Haunted Houses

One very popular image that is conjured up by the word **ghost** is an old abandoned house with loose, banging shutters and doors that seem to be closed by some unseen hand. To a certain extent, this stereotype is justified, for houses are the favorite hangouts of ghosts. Generally, the houses are not abandoned, and in most narratives, no mention is made of the size of the residence. Usually the haunting is done by male ghosts, but neither are female ghosts rare. The haunting usually takes place in communities that have a long history of settlement and a relatively stable population. As the following selections illustrate, ghosts haunt houses for various reasons and, in most cases, are not harmful to human beings although they may often prove to be a nuisance. A few Southern ghosts have no specific motivation, but these purposeless wraiths are rare.

The first story given here appears in this section rather than in that on witches only because the informant called it a ghost story. Nevertheless, many of the incidents that occur in this narrative are commonly encountered not only in Southern ghostlore but in that of the United States. The narrative featuring the supernatural antics of Sally Carter is a good example of a tale in which the ghost returns not for just a single reason but for several. The story about Sam Graves is one of many Southern legends involving the ghostly reenactment of a murder. Another text reveals the story of a young *suicide who refuses to leave the house where she died; presumably, she is unable to rest in her grave because she ended her life prematurely. Other stories in this section include one about a haunted bed in which no one can sleep, another concerning an ineradicable bloodstain, several concerning strange ghostly noises, and one about a ghost that pulled cover from the bed where people were sleeping.*

Here, then, are some typical Southern ghosts. They usually return for some specific reason that is often revealed in the course of the narrative, although in some cases it never comes clear. In every case, their story is of more than passing interest.

1 ☠

Uncle I.H. decided to build a house for his nephew. The plans were drawn and soon some itinerant carpenters and painters came along to help in the construction and painting of the house. The nephew, Mr. S., lived in a log cabin just back of the construction site. An agreement was reached whereby the itinerant workers could sleep in the new building and board with the S. family. Mr. S., his wife and small daughter lived in the cabin. One day, as the house neared completion, one of the carpenters walked in and told Mr. S. that he was leaving the job because someone had put a hex on the place and he could not sleep at night for all the noise going on in the new house. The doors opened and closed all night, there was a tapping sound in the walls, strange things were happening in the hallway. Mr. S. assured him that in all probability some of the neighborhood boys were ticktacking the house; he would therefore clean up the debris that very day and would in all probability solve the mystery. True to his promise, he cleaned the house and surrounding premises that day, but he failed to find the ticktacking evidence. Mr. S. decided that he and his wife and child could move in the new structure and all this foolishness would stop.

Unfortunately, this did not give the carpenter peace of mind, nor did it help the S. family. At night they would see a casket roll up to the side of their bed. They would light a lamp and there would be nothing there. As they would try to settle down again, their bed would rise from the floor. The house moaned and creaked all night long. The wagon belonging to the little girl raced up and down the center hallway. The doors opened and closed all night.

Mr. S. watched the workmen closely and came to the conclusion that the painter was the offending person with devilish powers. He confronted him with this information, and the painter acknowledged that he was possessed with powers from the devil and every night before he went to sleep he released these evil spirits to do their work.

One day Mr. S. had to go to town, and Mrs. S. prepared dinner as was her custom and called the workmen in to eat. The painter in question asked her how she would like to see her kitchen table start walking. She was frightened but rather sternly replied that if he wanted to keep eating there, he had better leave his tricks away from the kitchen.

The house was eventually completed, and as the painter took his departure, he was warned that he had better take his evil spirits away with him. He departed, but it was noted that doors in the house, closed and latched they might be, without warning would come open and be standing ajar.

This house was eventually partially burned, and in its place a new house was constructed. The only part of the old building put in the new was the front door. The new front door could be latched, firmly closed, but with no warning could come open. Mrs. B. and her family all believe this is the ghost of the devil-possessed painter still doing his work.

2 ☠

Well anyway, that first summer we were there we would all be out in the field working, and Momma would be there at the house, and her first grandchild, Leontine, would be there with her, and Momma said the first time she noticed anything she thought she heard a bunch of people coming up out front talking and she wondered who could that be, because she knew it wasn't time for us to come from the field for dinner, and she went out, looked everywhere and didn't see a soul. Well, that's the first thing she told us when we came to the house for dinner, that she heard noises, and she thought it was somebody coming up out front. Well, she didn't see anything. So it went like that and...one Saturday night Louie and Beulah came to stay all night with us, and that left Mildred and me to sleep upstairs, and after the lights were out, well, we were lying there in bed and all of a sudden my cover began to move off of me and I told her, "Stop pulling all the cover!" And she said, "Sister, I'm not pulling the cover," and I knew she wasn't because she was perfectly still. Well, next thing we knew we were rolling downstairs. It scared us.

Well anyway, Louie was there from the time we moved in until the next October he married. And he slept up there one night and he was the first one that told us the cover slid off him, and we knew very well there wasn't anybody up there. Well, we didn't go back up there to sleep anymore. So that went on, oh, I don't know, a long time. We didn't go back up there to sleep anymore. Papa tried to get us to, but we told him he could if he wanted to but we wouldn't.

So then that fall, we started to school, and the school building was close, where we walked, and in the evenings there was a little pond—We had to pass this pond coming from the school to the house, and I happened to look up at the upstairs window, and until today I can see that; it looked like a big, a huge Newfoundland—what do you call these dogs, not a Newfoundland but a St. Bernard. It looked just like a huge St. Bernard dog reared up to that window and just as plain as if I'd been standing there. Well, Sook saw it too. We both did. I said, "Look," and she looked and there was that dog. It looked just like a big St. Bernard dog reared up to that window. Well, it was after that in the evenings when we'd come home and get along by this pond, I don't know why we didn't hear anything or see anything until we'd get near this pond. Then we'd hear an organ start playing "Nearer My God To Thee." Nana, that's absolutely the truth, and if Mildred were here she'd tell you the same thing. Well, it just excited us so that we didn't know whether something had happened to Momma or what. We were just almost afraid to go to the house.

We were all excited and telling Momma about it, and she kind of laughed it off. Then she got to telling us about hearing those voices more than once. She said she'd gone out of the house to look and see who was coming up out front. Well, it went on like that, and then in the wintertime one Sunday night my boyfriend was there, and he and Mildred and I were sitting in front of the fire, and we knew this spinning wheel was upstairs but we knew there wasn't anybody up there because Momma and Papa and Jake were in the other room, and it was in the winter and that spinning wheel started a'spinning. Oh, it sounded like you'd gone and taken your finger, you know, like you spin a wheel to and it would stop on a certain number. It just spun and just roared, it ran so fast. Well, this boyfriend of mine, he said, "What's that?" We told him, "It, well, they always said it was Mr. Yancey upstairs." That's what Emma, everybody around said. We weren't the only ones that ever heard it either.

Then Momma had a wire clothesline up there where she hung her clothes in the winter, and that thing...One night this same fellow was there, and it sounded like you had taken your finger and pulled that wire down tight and turned it loose and it made a funny noise again, and I was telling Jim about it this morning, and he said, "Do you actually believe in all of that?"

I said, "Well, if he was here, he could tell you the same thing, but he can't be here to tell you because he's dead."

Oh, and again it was in the wintertime, and Mildred and I had gone to bed, and then, well, she and I all the time slept across the hall from where Momma and Papa slept. We'd gone to bed and was just lying there talking and whenever we closed the door that went into the hall, and we heard this noise, and you know how a dog—when he has run quite a distance and when he gets hot—how he will lap his tongue, you know, and make the noise, and that was the same kind of sound we heard. It came out of the hall and you could hear it. It sounded like you could hear his claws hooking in the carpet as it went across. It went to the big fireplace and just disappeared. And we jerked the covers over our heads, and I don't know how long we kept the cover over our heads, we were so scared. But finally when I got nerve enough, I eased the cover back and I called for Papa and told him what we'd heard, and I said, "Light the lamp and bring it in here." Well, he or Momma one lighted the lamp, but they didn't come across that hall. We rolled out of that bed and went across that hall and we didn't go back in there that night either.

And that's the only time we ever heard that. But we kidded Momma and Papa about being afraid. They were scared too, and I don't know whether they had heard noises in the house either, but…We lived there three years, and we heard things once in a great while. But he always said it was the rats running across the floor upstairs.

---

3 ☠

When my granddaddy bought that place down here, why, they moved over from the other side of the mountain. And so they had a lot of stuff to move. They brought over a load or two of stuff, two wagonfuls, and brought some of the women over and they stayed all night. Well, the menfolks went back 'cross the mountain fer to get some more furniture and stuff. Well, there was three women, I think. They was kinda brave. So they brought lard and all kinda groceries and stuff, you know, fer to have, and that's what they brought with the first load. So they had a great big dog they brought along with 'em for these women to keep with 'em if anything bothered 'em.

They said they had a big jar, a big stone jar, and they had lard in that and they put it in that big press back in that room. They put this lard and some meat and stuff in thar. Well, the women stayed thar that night, and the menfolks went on back over the mountain to get another load. So they said way in the night then they heerd sump'n fall in the dining room 'bout that old closet, 'bout that press whar they put the lard and stuff. One of these women said to the other one, says, "Lawd have mercy," says, "let's get up and go in thar." Says, "That dog I bet done knocked that big jar of lard over." And they got up and lit the lamp and went in thar, and the door was fastened to the press and everything, wasn't no lard out nor dog wasn't in thar nor nothing. And when they come thar they had back in that hall a part where they used to keep the saddle under the stairsteps.

And I heerd my granddaddy, after he lived down thar, said they could hear 'em go out thar every night and draggin', you know, taking the saddle out, you know, and hearing the belly cinch and the buckle part, you know, dragging across the floor when they went on out the door, went on down the steps. Had the saddle on their arm and the buckle on the belly banging over, dragging on the floor. Said they heerd that and they went in thar to see if somebody got the saddle or was going out. Some of the boys, they's always going out a'riding, trying to catch a horse after night. Thar's the saddle and all back in thar just like they'd left it.

---

4 💀

In 1826, Mary Carter was married and moved there (to the house in Huntsville, Alabama). In 1836, Sally, who was Mary's sister, came to visit. There she caught the whooping cough and died. She is buried in the family cemetery. Before my grandmother moved there, two other families owned it and in between the house was unoccupied for long periods of time. They moved there in 1919, and the woman who was moving out told them to not let Sally's tombstone get toppled over.

So one time, my grandparents were having a party and they invited a whole bunch of people and they had to stay overnight. So my cousin Charles Martin had to sleep in the upstairs hall.

During the night a storm came up, and he looked out over the balcony and saw a ghost standing there. She had long blonde hair, and she had on a long white robe, and she walked very softly through the screen door and sat down on the inside. She put her hand on his forehead and said, "Will you please help me? A tree has knocked my tombstone over." So the next day, Charles got up and told everybody what happened, and he finally got my grandfather and some more men to go over to the cemetery, and the tombstone was toppled over. So they put it back up. They thought Charles had dreamed it all up; they didn't think it was any big deal.

After that—my daddy and my aunt grew up in that room—and after they left, this man moved in, he rented the house from my grandmother. He was a very heavy chainsmoker, and Sally didn't like it. You know she didn't like smoke, because every time somebody was smoking she would slam doors and things like that.

I've heard that on her grave the headstone fell over, and every time they put it up it falls back over. It won't stand up for anything. If you stand on her grave at night she will haunt you that night, she will follow you home. This friend of mine heard that she was in love with this guy and he didn't love her back, so she jumped off that balcony into a rosebush. You hear all kinds of stories—and they just get bigger and bigger—that really didn't happen.

5 ☠

There is this house in San Elizario that's haunted. But he's a funny ghost that haunts it—he only likes women. If a girl goes into the house, he pinches her. The house belongs to some people named Lujan. I think they were related to me. Anyway, they all died.

Some people moved into the house. The ghost kept bothering the wife—pinching her. They didn't like it, so they moved out. Some more people moved in. The ghost pinched this wife too. When they went to bed she could feel the ghost feeling her and rubbing his hands on he legs. But they got used to the ghost.

Why don't you go see for yourself?

6 ☠

One evening on a little farm out west of Warren, Sam Graves sat down at his kitchen table to have supper. For reasons unknown, he and his wife had been having trouble. Before Sam had a chance to help his plate, his wife, who had prepared the nice supper, walked up behind him with a rifle and shot him point-blank in the upper part of his back. Stunned, Sam slumped over the table, filling the plate before him with blood. Then he rose to his feet, staggered across the room out the front door and sat down on the front porch steps. His wife dropped the single-shot rifle and grabbed up the butcher knife from the table. She ran out to where her bleeding and stunned husband sat and started stabbing him repeatedly with the knife. Once again, Sam got up and half stumbled, half crawled out to the orchard and died.

This happened in 1922. Mrs. Graves had been apprehended and executed. The little farmhouse stood untouched for many years. Everything was left just as it was the evening of the murder. Even the dried-up blood stains were still in the plate on the table. But years later, a member of a logging crew swore he heard a shot come from the house as he was walking by the vicinity. He was alone, but he went in the house to investigate. He was horrified when he saw the plate on the kitchen table filled with fresh blood. At first, people back in Warren thought he was crazy. The logger took some men back out to the haunted farm, but all they found was a plate of dried blood looking like it had for years.

But people changed their minds when they realized it had been exactly ten years to the day since Sam Graves had been murdered. Still today, many people who remember the incident believe that Sam Graves gets murdered again and again on that horrible anniversary.

7 ☠

This is a personal account of a ghost story that occurred a little more than forty years ago, and at that time the house which I visited had been empty some three or four years. I was staying at the Edgewater Beach Hotel on the Gulf Coast with my Aunt Harriet, who was a professional journalist. She was editor of a paper at that time; until 1959 she held that position. She was a woman of truth, integrity…and she didn't hold much with ghosts, but we made this excursion at the specific request of a friend of hers whose house this was.

The friends had been long-time friends of hers, and they owned a large plantation-type home on the Gulf, but they had not been able to live in it for several years because their daughter, who had been a teenager, had committed suicide in the house and her ghost was reported to haunt the house. At any rate, late one evening after dinner and moving well past my bedtime, we got into the car and drove down toward the beach with Aunt Harriet's instructions that we were going to examine something that she considered to be a phenomenon, and that although she didn't believe in ghosts, there were some unusual occurrences taking place in this house, and we were just going to see what *was* there. And then, she was going to report back to the parents and tell them that obviously there was no such thing as a ghost there, and that it was all right, but we were supposed to be able to explain what was occurring at the house.

So we drove up to the house and entered it with the key Aunt Harriet had gotten from her friends, and we arranged chairs in the front hallway, and we sat there quietly for some time. It must have been more than an hour, and I suppose the appropriate witching hour, which should have been midnight, had gotten close. But I really don't have much concept of time because I was a child and because one doesn't have much concept of time when one is just sitting in an empty house waiting on something to happen. But along about what I suppose to be midnight, we heard a noise in the upstairs hall and it sounded distinctly like footsteps, and the footsteps came out of a bedroom and closed a door and then proceeded to come down the hall, and my eyes went to the top of the stairs, and although the light inside the house was very dim, I expected to be able to see a figure standing at the top of the stairs. Of course, I did not. The steps hesitated for a moment and then continued to come down the stairs slowly but steadily, and as the steps got toward the foot of the steps, which were directly in front of me, I could see, even in the dim light, a depression in the carpet, and then the steps touched the marble hallway and clicked across the foyer and then went back down the hall just a little way toward the double music-room doors, and those doors opened.

Naturally, I was terrified, but I looked to Aunt Harriet to see what she was doing, and she was sitting perfectly still, and I knew that I should sit perfectly still too. So, we watched the doors open and heard the steps continue across the floor until they came to the piano, which was within our vision with those double doors open. We watched as the piano stool came back. The top to the piano was raised—the keyboard—and then, after a few moments, assuming that this person, whoever it was, was arranging themselves at the stool and in front of the keyboard, began to play and continued to play through about three pieces of Chopin, and then the music stopped, the keyboard was lowered. The piano bench went back, and we heard the steps come back out of the room. The double doors were closed and then...*tap*...the steps tapped again across the marble foyer and touched the bottom of the steps, where they hesitated as though whoever it was that was performing for us was watching *us* or looking at us, because they turned. Poised for a moment and then went up the steps...back up the hallway upstairs, went back into the bedroom, and the door was closed.

That was the end of what was, for me at least, a singular event. And Aunt Harriet said, "It's now time to go." So we closed the house up and left, got back into the car, and on the way back into town, I asked her if this was indeed the ghost and if this was the girl who was supposed to have killed herself and was now haunting the house and if this was why the parents couldn't stay there anymore. And she told me with one line, and that was the last one on the subject, "There is no such thing as a ghost."

8 ☠

Well, one night I went down to my cousin's to stay all night. We set around and talked for a while after supper, telling tales and jokes. 'Long toward bedtime they ast me where I wanted to sleep. I said that if hit made no difference, I was gonna sleep in that danged hainted bed back in t'other room. They tried awful hard to argy me out of it, but I uz long, long headed and finally had my way. We went in and I looked all around to see that there wasn't anybody who uz gonna pull a trick on me. Then they went on back in the other room, and I shucked off my clothes and crawled in bed. I hadn't more'n got fixed when sumpin down at the footboard began to pull the kivver; it would pull it down and I'd pull it back. Well, I got tired of that and give a big jerk. That hadn't more'n happened when every quilt on the bed sailed right over the foot of that bed. "Bring in a lamp," sez I, "some danged fool's trying to play a trick on me." In they came with a lamp, but there was the room jist as empty as a ol' bee gum. Nobody could've gotten in or out either. They begged me agin to come on and sleep in the "big house" where they was, 'cause nobody ever could sleep on that bed. "Lemme try it agin," sez I. They agreed. So I rolled up in the kivver and hugged up to the feather bed and straw bed, and then, *wham*, the whole kerpoodle landed right over on the floor, straw bed, feather bed and all. When they come runnin' in with the lamp, there set that bed a'trembling like a leaf. No sir, I didn't sleep on it and ain't nobody else ever slept on it either. That bed was hainted shore's you're born.

9 ☠

You mean that place down in the holler? Lord, yes, hit's haunted, allers has been as fur back as I kin recollect. I don't know whur ye'd call hit a hant er not. Hit's a sort of evil sperit that hangs over hit all the time. Wuzn't ye never inside of hit? Well, ef ye'll go and look, ye'll find a powerful red stain on the floor, right behind the front door. I ain't never knowed nobody that lived thar sence Jim and Allie Honeycutt moved out. She said that as long as she lived thar that no matter how hard she'd scrub that place with soap and water hit wuld jest git brighter, ever time, and hit never would come off. I never knowed how that red stain got thar, but Pap, he allers 'lowed that some pore feller wuz kilt thar in time of the war. Ye know they say that at one time they wuz a gang of robbers had their den thar, and they'd go out and git people, lettin' on like they wuz friendly to 'em and nobody would ever know what went with 'em.

Nobody ever lives thar now because as shore as they do, they's some member of their family certain to die. Ye know Little Joe Dugger, he moved his family in thar and 'lowed he'd live thar. But they warn't thar no time till their gal tuck sick with the fever, and the raincrows and screech owls, hit was a sight to hear 'em. They jist kept on a'hollerin' till she died, and then they jist kep up their lonesome croakin' till Milly, she jist told Joe that they wuz all a'goin' to die ef they didn't git away from thar, and they moved out.

Then Jim Honeycutt, ye know he lived thar fur awhile and his little boy died. Allie said hit wuz a fever, and I don't know what hit wuz. 'Peared to me like hit wuz some kind o' curious trouble that jist come up outer the ground. Everybody that I've ever heard tell of that lived thar allers had trouble. Some of their folks wuz shore to die. Don't I remember the night that Abe Canter's wife died? They wuz a'livin' right thar in that house. Bob and me set up till twelve, and that night I had a dream. I dreamt that this here yard all around here wuz all lit up, jist as ef hit wuz a fire, and I looked agin and I seed a white angel a'comin' and hit jist floated down right easy, jist like a soap bubble when hit's in the air before hit gits busted. Then hit looked at me with hits face jist a'shinin' and hit pinted hits finger at me, and hit says, "Ye've been a'sinnin'." Yes hit did! Hit says, "Ye've been a'sinnin'," jist as plain as me a'speakin' to you, and I says, "Yes," says I, "I've been a'sinnin'."

Then hit looked at me agin, hit did, and hit says, "Go and sin no more!" Yes hit did. Then I waked up, I did, and I still seed that angel plain as day. So I jist punched Bob and I says, "Bob," says I, "Hit's sin, jist sin, that's caused hit all."

10 ☠

The next story is about a hainted house that was near a cave, in this vicinity. The old house had been there ever since before the Civil War. And people lived in it all of this time. And there was a place way back in the mountains, still of course—the place is still there. There is no house or anything. It was called the old Russian place. They're supposed to have a lot of money buried up there. And the man that buried the money had killed a man and took his wife. All the men nearby were gone to war. This was during the Civil War. So he did all of this and he kept the money. And everybody wondered where it was. And everybody tried to find it and nobody could. But they moved to this house, down closer to other people, this old Linebarger house I call it. And they just kinda took over where they lived, nobody bothered them much because he was kind of a bad man.

And the man that got killed had a son, and he had been off in the war. He came back, and all of this had happened. Of course, he didn't like that, and he decided he'd just get even with the guy. So he just sent him word that he was going to kill him. Well, the old man didn't believe him.

But early one morning someone knocked on the door. The woman went to see who it was. And it was before the man got up. They had a big old room, they had this bed in the room, and there was a big fireplace, big rock hearth—the fireplace was rock—and a big mantle. This man, this young man came in. She screamed, and he came on in. And the old man was in the bed, just lying there. And he saw who it was. And he said, "Get out of bed, I am going to kill you." He had his gun in his hand. The man that was in the bed had his gun under his pillow. He went for his gun. The man shot at him, missed, and the bullet went into the mantle, under the rock, and it went into this piece of wood. And the man that was in the bed raised up, grabbed his gun. But before he could do all of that, the guy shot again, shot him right in the forehead. He fell back dead.

Well, of course, there was never anything done about that either that I ever heard of. And I don't think there was anyone who ever said there was. But they took him and buried him. And they never did bother to take the bullet out of this mantle. Now I seen that place, many times. And this bullet stayed there just for people to show off, until the house burned several years later.

But after that the house got hainted. Now strange things happened there, so they said. Sometimes someone would knock on the door, and it would open; you'd go see who it was, there wasn't a soul there. But it would sound like they would step right in the room. People thought it was the ghost of this man who came to kill this man who was in the bed. Then, sometimes, the back door would open. And they'd have to go close the door. They told all kinds of things, you could hear a man walking sometimes across the room just like the man that opened the door. Maybe he'd come from the back and he'd walk across the room and out the front door. But you wouldn't see a thing.

This went on for many years. But finally the house burned; after that, nobody ever saw the ghost. This house was located right close to a cave. Whether that had anything to do with it I do not know.

11

I was never afraid of haunts in my life. And when we moved up there to a house near Prestonburg, Kentucky, why the house had been empty a long time. I didn't know what was wrong. I just thought he couldn't rent it, you know. And I went out to my neighbor's house, and she said, "Do you know that that house is haunted?"

I said, "No, I didn't know it."

"Well, it is, and you'll soon know it."

Well, it wasn't very long until, sure enough, it come. They was in the hall—one of my little girls was in the hall. We had a hall in the house. She was in there, and this other one was between the dining room, and she went out to the backyard. And so it knocked on the door, just as hard as it could knock. She said to the other girl, "You couldn't scare me." She thought it was her, trying to scare her. Then she looked out there and seen her shrieking and she went out there to tell her about it, and while she was telling her about it, why the table turned over and broke all the things it seemed like we had in the world. Broke all the dishes and everything else. When I come back they was settin' over at the barn. I said, "Children, what in the world's the matter?"

"Oh, Mama," they said, "everything we got's broke. Everything on earth we got."

And I went over there, and they was just like they was when I left. They wasn't turned over, nor nothin' bothered at all. And that's the way it was. I knowed the house was haunted, but I never could see nothin' myself. It scared the children to death, but it never bothered me. I'd go out in the night and get coal. 'Way in the night, to the coal house. And I'd go down in the cellar. And I never could see nothin'. I'd think about it...and I never could see a thing. It never come when I was there, either—only when I was gone. And you know we stayed there two year and I wasn't afraid.

---

12 💀

The mode of travel back then was by horseback or on foot. This particular man was walking with a pack on his back, and around dusk became tired so he stopped at an old two-room shack to spend the night. But before he entered the old shack he happened to notice that there were nine unmarked graves at the back of the shack.

He hesitated about staying all night, but he was so tired he lay down in one of the rooms to get a night's rest. But all of a sudden he heard voices in the next room who said, "Sharpen the knife, this one will make ten." The voices were eerie but came clearly from the next room. He was carrying a gun, so he burst into the other room, but to his amazement only a flickering candle was on the floor and nothing else. He ran out of the house until he came to a house down the road and told his story to the people living there. They said, "Oh! that old shack has been empty for years, we call it the haunted house of the nine graves."

13 💀

José was very sad. His wife had just been buried, and now he was alone.

"Poor José, you are very silent. Can I help you?" said Donaciana.

José looked up and saw his neighbor. She had brought him some food and flowers.

Soon after this, José fell in love with the kind Donaciana and married her.

One hot night, José slept outside in the moonlight. Donaciana had gone to visit her sister in a neighboring village, leaving Jose alone. All at once he began to shiver. Something cold was pressing his feet. He was almost paralyzed with fright. Maria's ghost stood at the foot of his cot. It was her hands that were pressing his feet.

With a yell, he ran into the house and barred the door.

After a sleepless night, José went to the village with his story.

"My son, do not be afraid. Maria was a good woman. She means you no harm. When she comes again, ask her what it is that she wants from you," said the kindly priest.

José thanked him and returned to his home.

That night José slept outside again. When he felt cold hands grip his feet he said, "Maria, what do you wish of me?"

"José, I am glad that you are happy, but I cannot rest in peace. I owe the grocer, Xavier, *seis pesetas,* and I cannot rest in peace until you pay the debt. Give him the money, José, and let me rest peacefully."

In the morning, Xavier's first visitor was José. He paid the *pesetas* and was never again troubled by Maria's ghost.

14 ☠

Well, I'll tell you one experience. We were right down here to Headquarters. My daughter-in-law what was with me tonight, well, that was her homeplace. We were settin' up there with her mother one night just before she died. Her sister were there and had a cot there, and I was sittin' 'side the bed where the lady was layin' and I was wipin' the sweat off her and givin' her cold water. There was a big door right there, and the wind were just as still and calm as it could be. All at once that door flew wide open, and the lady and her sister layin' over there, and another lady was settin' over in a chair kindly dozin'. And I reckon it was around twelve o'clock in the night. We was settin' there. That door flew wide open. So her sister got up and she shet that door, and when she turned her back that door flew wide open agin. Wasn't a piece of wind anywhere a'blowin'. Well, I said to the neighbor settin' there, I said, "Well, what do you think of that?"

She said, "I don't know." Said, "There's not a piece of wind."

We sit there. So I got up then and went in the kitchen and got a cup of coffee and came back. Dinin' room right over there. The little hall right in that way where you go in the livin' room. Dinin' room right there. 'Twas prompt twelve o'clock. We were settin' there. Just had the light turned down low because the lady was ill. We 'as lookin' for her to pass on any minute. All at once we heered the pot tops just a'rattlin' in the dinin' room, and I knew they had cleaned up already. Had a long table, oh, the table were long because they had so many, you know, to eat when they were younger people and they never did smallen the table down. The pot tops and the lids just rattled. And I thought to myself, "Well, I just wonder who that is in there in the pots."

So the lady was settin' over there, and Mrs. Foster then were layin' over on the bed. I just kindly eased over to the door and I peeked around the door to see if I seen anybody, see if there were pots on the table. Wasn't no pots. Table settin' just like they'd left it. We could hear the pot lids. Hear 'em when they take 'em off and hear 'em when they put 'em back. I set myself down, and all at once it looked like they brought in 'bout a dishpan full of knives and forks and spoons and dumped 'em over in the middle of the table. You never heerd such a fuss in your life. And it was even twelve o'clock, but you could see that house there used to keep slaves there, you see, and I told the lady there, I said, "I reckon the pore old slaves is gettin' the tables all ready for 'em to eat." I said,

"The pots is rattlin', the lids is rattlin', even poured out the knives and forks on top of the table."

That's 'fore the lady died. She died next morning, nine o'clock. I said, "Well sir," I said, "I don't believe daylight'll ever come tonight." I waited till four o'clock in the mornin' before I left down the road by myself. Yes sir, when daylight did come, I moved it on home. And the girl here, one of 'em, sent word over there for me to come back over there, that their mother had passed on. Well, her mother, when she died, I was settin' up there with her, and so when they laid her out over in the parlor room, her brother was there, and the whole house was settin' full of people. So they was a man and his wife was from up there, and I used to work with 'em in the orchard, and I were tellin' him about hearin' things. He looked at me and he said, "I wish I could hear sump'n. It wouldn't scare me a bit."

I said, "I wish you could hear sump'n too and see what I see."

So 'long about 'leven o'clock, here us just the neighbors settin' up in this room, and my daughter-in-law's mother layin' 'cross the hall in the parlor room, and her brother and her sister-in-law was settin' there in the floor. All at once we heard the awfullest noise fall. We thought the casket had fell off the stand in the floor. And her brother jumped up with his flashlight and said, "Law," said, "sister's casket has fell off."

Well, he run with the flashlight—we didn't have 'lectric lights then like we have now—he run with his flashlight, and we all follered him, and when we got into the parlor room there set the casket just like the undertakers had set it. But we couldn't give no 'count. We could even feel the floor jar across that hall and into the settin' room that we was settin'. Look like you could feel the floor kindly shake. Right there at Headquarters.

Lord, man, I could just set and talk all night about them ghost tales. We just heerd those things down there and I told Lucille, I said, "I wouldn't stay there by myself." Oh, there was ghosts always seen down there.

15 🕱

I was at my girlfriend's house one day and decided to spend the night. Her grandmother, who was dead, had been crippled and walked with a limp. That night, when everybody was asleep, we all heard footsteps in the house. (My friend's mother told us what happened to her in the morning.) The footsteps went through the kitchen, into the bathroom and into my friend's mother's bedroom. As the footsteps walked, we heard a limp—*da dum da dum.*

In the morning, her mother told us that in the night she had heard the footsteps also. Then she suddenly had sensed that somebody was behind her. Suddenly, she felt a hand on her shoulder! She began to pray very hard. She was so frightened and was praying so hard that she finally fell asleep.

Later in the day, we were all in the kitchen talking. It was in the winter, and there was snow outside. I smelled the scent of perfume in the kitchen and asked who had put it on. Everybody said that it wasn't them. Then it seemed to fade away as if it were going another way. Then it came back.

My friend then reminded me that she had told me that her grandmother often came to visit them. They could tell she was there because of the perfume she was wearing. No one else in the house used that scent of perfume. When they smelled this scent, they would know that she had come for a visit. The second time I smelled the scent, it was so strong, like it was standing right next to me. It was weird! I got scared and left.

16 ☠

I used to play tennis in a park in an older section of El Dorado. There was a house across the street, owned by H.L. Hunt. The house and grounds took up an entire city block. By the time I was playing tennis in the park in the '60s, no one lived in the house. There were signs around the house saying "KEEP OUT," but it was always fun to go sneaking around somewhere you weren't supposed to be.

I think any old house left empty for a number of years assumes a story or legend. Someone will go in and hear noises and some kind of a legend will grow out of it. This is the way legends are made. I don't think the legend things you hear are true. There might be some small thing of truth in it, but it is blown way out of proportion.

Anyway, the story about this house was something like a party going on at the house. Hunt's girlfriend was there, and she fell down the stairs and broke her neck. When you go in the house and hear these noises, people think it is Hunt's girlfriend coming back looking for him.

The house was torn down several years ago.

17 ☠

My mom and dad used to live in Paragould. Mother says it was real weird. The house had a creepy upstairs that they never used. The stairway came down in the dining room. Mom had a dark green curtain hanging at the end. Every night when they would go to bed, they heard someone walking up and down the stairs for about twenty minutes. Daddy looked a couple of times and didn't find anything.

Later they heard the lady that lived there before them used to walk those stairs for exercise every night before bed. People said that she had left a lot of cats behind, and the cats were looking for the woman. My mom got so scared after that that she used to follow Daddy to the field.

It went on for about forty-five minutes one night. Daddy was determined to do something. He got a flashlight and a gun and went to the stairs. When he pulled back the curtain, something jumped out on him. They looked all through the house and didn't find a thing.

Later, cats started showing up all over town. No one knew where they were coming from. Then Mom saw a cat on the eating table. She swears it was a strange cat. Some time later they found out the lady had died in Little Rock. The cats were searching for her spirit. My mother really believes that.

18 ☠

My parents lived in a haunted house right after they were married. A man froze to death in the house about four or five months before they moved there. They said when it started turning cold that people began to talk.

Well, the first night it snowed they got in a disagreement about hogging the cover. Every morning at breakfast they would accuse each other of taking all the cover during the night. One night before they went to sleep, the cover began to move. Mom said something to Dad. He said, "Me?" The cover was being pulled off at the foot of the bed.

The next day they started looking for a house. It took them awhile to find another place. That was the only thing they noticed. They talked to the thin air at night. They said they would talk, and the cover would move different ways.

I'm getting married during Christmas. We have rented an older type here in Jonesboro. I'm sort of wary.

2 Other Haunted Places

Although old houses are the favorite hangout for ghosts, the otherworldly creatures can be found haunting just about any place. In American tradition, they frequently haunt battlefields, mines, highways, boats, graveyards, gallows and wells.

In the stories that follow, ghosts haunt a tree where a youth was executed by guerrillas, battlefields, hollows, a mill, a lake, a courthouse, a rock, cemeteries, a college and a casketmaker's shop. They haunt these places for various reasons including unjust execution, suicide, restless souls, a desire to eternally torture their victims, as a sign of divine retribution, to complete business left unfinished at the time of their death, or because they have forgotten something and are returning to find it.

These varied reasons are the ones most commonly found in Southern tradition. The ghost tales recounted here range in age from the Revolutionary War up to the present time. As with most ghosts, these are generally more of a nuisance than they are harmful.

19 ☠

Gold Hill lifts its peaks far above the fertile valleys of eastern Forsyth County. On the tiptop is a large opening, now crowded with debris and undergrowth, its rocky, perpendicular sides glazed by wind and rain. This is the deserted gold mine that still holds the spirit of Elizabeth Reed. Every time the wind whips around the crags and crevices, there issues from the depths of the pit an agonizing wail. Sometimes it is the faint wail of a child. Then again, it is the shriek of a woman.

It was during the Revolutionary War that Richard Reed was killed in a battle with the British, and his wife, Elizabeth, went mad.

One day Elizabeth sat crouched in her chair watching her grandmother prepare the noonday meal. As the old woman busied herself between the table and fireplace, Elizabeth's eyes took on a deep cunning. She hated the old woman who watched her every move and hated the squalling baby that lay in the cradle. She hated everyone except Richard, her husband the British had killed.

But that wasn't true. Richard wasn't dead. The old woman was keen. She had hidden Richard in the deserted mine on the top of Gold Hill and was leaving him there to starve. The night before, an owl had sat in the tree beside her window and told her all about it. It told her that the old woman had tied Richard's hands and feet, then flung him into the pit, but that he wasn't dead and that she could get him out if she did as the owl told her.

Elizabeth's hands began to move. She plucked at her sleeves and gnawed her nails, all the time watching Old Granny through slitted lids. How ugly she was with her gray hair straggling down the back of her neck and her skin the color of a tanned rawhide! And the baby was no better. Elizabeth turned her gaze to the child in the cradle. It was a squirming piece of flesh that only ate and cried. She would far rather have a rabbit that was woolly and soft. She despised the baby, she wanted nothing but Richard, and she was going to have him. The owl had told her if she threw her baby into the Gold Hill mine that Old Granny would give her Richard, so as soon as she could slip the baby away, she was going to fling him into the mine; then Richard would be hers again.

Elizabeth turned her gaze back to Old Granny. She stood facing the table, kneading dough. There was flour on her blue-checked gingham apron and a fine dust showed on her yellow arms. Elizabeth rose quietly from her chair. Noiseless and swift as a cat, she darted across the room to the baby's cradle, reaching out her hands for him. Just as she touched him, she saw the old woman turn and rush toward her.

"There, there," she heard Granny say, "don't you worry, Lizzie. You just sit quiet and rest. Granny will take care of little Richard."

Elizabeth sank back in her chair, her eyes gleaming balefully. That was always the way. They wouldn't let her get her hands on the child. She knew what they were thinking, Granny and the neighbors too. They thought she was crazy, but she wasn't; it was Granny who was crazy. The owl told her so, and the bird told her that Granny was keeping the baby from her, just as she was keeping Richard from her. Elizabeth held up her hands and began awkwardly to count her fingers. She lowered her lids to keep from seeing Old Granny, who had moved to the other side of the table and stood facing her, alert and watchful. Suddenly Granny gave a cry and rushed to the door, looking out into the garden.

"The calf!" she cried. "It's in the garden eating the peas!" She ran out across the yard, calling to the calf.

For a moment Elizabeth sat motionless, and her eyes began to glitter. She leaped from the chair and ran to the cradle. Snatching up the child, she dashed out the back door and into the woods, fleet as a deer. As she passed the spring beneath the sycamores, her laughter broke, shattering into a shrill, vibrating echo that floated out behind her, reaching the ears of Old Granny, who was tying the calf.

Elizabeth climbed the steep incline nimbly. She was free at last, free with the baby they wouldn't allow her to touch. She was going to do as the owl said, take the baby to the mine on top of Gold Hill and fling it down into the dark depths. Then Old Granny would free Richard and give him back to her. Higher and higher she went. The trees pressed close about her; the thorns of the bayberry vines tore her face and arms, leaving bright crimson streaks, and the sharp stones in the narrow path bruised and cut her bare feet, but she staggered on. She stopped, panting for breath, when a sound held her motionless.

Behind her was the sound of voices. Even as she stood quiet, a shout broke the stillness. It was Granny and Uncle Bill, the Negro who fed the horses, coming after her, but they mustn't catch her.

Hugging the baby tighter, she turned and sped up the last steep incline. It wasn't far now. Her breath came in short, broken gasps. Behind her she could hear the thudding sound of running feet and Old Granny calling her name, but she only ran faster. A minute now and she would be there. Already she could see the dark opening of the mine just a few feet ahead. With a last desperate effort she reached the hilltop.

At her feet the pit gaped wide open. Somewhere in that dark hole Richard was waiting, and in a few moments he would be with her. Leaning forward, she held the baby over the pit. As she did so, she heard the hoarse, panting cry of Old Granny, begging, pleading. The girl began to laugh, wild shrill laughter that stabbed the stillness of the forest with bloodcurdling mockery. She raised the child high above her head and flung it far out into space, watching it fall down, down, into the blackness of the mine. Then she whirled and faced Old Granny, who reached her, grasping her arm a moment too late.

Elizabeth continued to laugh as Old Granny fell on her knees, gazing frantically down into the mine. She watched with burning eyes as Uncle Bill fastened a rope to a tree, dropped it into the opening and clambered down. She even began to sing, a chanting tune of exultation. He was going after Richard. Soon she would see him again and they would be happy. The owl was right; Richard hadn't been shot in the war. He was alive and down in the mine where Granny had left him to starve. She moved nearer the opening and peered in, watching the Negro as he came slowly upward.

What was that he had in his arms? It was too small for Richard. As he drew nearer her face whitened; her lips drew back against her teeth and her eyes flamed beneath her frowsy hair. The man was bringing the baby back, a broken and bruised baby. She didn't want it; she wanted Richard. As the man reached the edge of the mine and climbed out and laid the lifeless child in Old Granny's arms, Elizabeth cowered back, watchful and sullen. So the old woman wasn't going to bring Richard out of the mine. She was going to keep him down there. Elizabeth chewed her lips, her hands plucked at each other. Then she slit a leaf to small fragments with her sharp nails, and a queer choking sound rattled in her throat. She would show Old Granny that she couldn't keep Richard imprisoned in the mine. She would go down into the pit herself and bring him out.

She moved forward, creeping craftily toward the rim of the pit, her eyes on the sobbing old woman who had forgotten her.

Slipping past Old Granny, Elizabeth reached the crumbling edge of the mine. For a moment she tottered there, leaning slightly forward, both hands clasped to her breast. Suddenly a wild, piercing cry tore from her throat. "Richard!" she screamed. "I see you. I'm coming!" Flinging her arms high, she leaped forward. For an instant her body hung suspended against the bright blue walls of the sky, then disappeared into the dark depths of the mine.

Today, when the wind beats against the crags of Gold Hill, wails still issue from the dark recesses of the old pit. Sometimes it is the agonizing wail of a child in pain, but more often it is the blood-curdling scream of a mad woman that echoes and re-echoes from the rocky, storm-glazed crevices of the mine—the mine that is still haunted by the spirit of Elizabeth Reed.

20 ☠

This was during the Civil War. And this was a big oak tree, stood on the side of a little country road that went through the country. And it had big limbs reaching out on all sides, kindly straight out. Not the kind of tree that the limbs point toward Heaven, the other kind, the kind you hang a man on. And in this community there lived a family and all of the people were gone to war except one boy, and he liked to speak his mind. But if you would keep your mouth shut you'd live longer; if people came by and they were for the North, then if you were for the South that caused trouble, and vicey versy. If you believed that other way around and they believed the other way around, you were just in for trouble.

This boy didn't mind to speak his piece. The jayhawkers came by, and, uh, he started to tell them off so they just took him out to this tree and hung him. People was afraid to go get him down, and he hung there all night long till the next day, and somebody had nerve enough to go and cut the rope, take him down and bury him.

Now for years and years this tree stood there. But it was hainted. They could see, on certain nights, an image of this boy hanging there on the tree. But it had a funny light around it. They all said they knew the boy went to Heaven because of this beautiful light they would see—they thought they could see—and that he had lived right and all of those things. But it got so people were afraid to go through the community where this was, where this tree was. Nobody had ever bothered to cut the tree down. It stayed there until, I suppose, it just died a natural death. But they always saw this boy, the image of this boy hanging from the tree.

21 ☠

One of the last battles was fought at Pleasant Hill, Louisiana. Great-Grandmother Mommom had moved to Pleasant Hill just after the Civil War was over. One day, Mommon and her sisters were crossing a field on which men had fought and she found a beautiful set of teeth, not false but real teeth. She took them home and put them in a box with some cotton. That night, Mommom, Great-Aunt Lottie and Jo Jo were sitting around the fire talking. Mommom looked up, and in the window she saw a face of a man. He had red-blond hair, awful eyes and blood all over him. She screamed and then fainted. After Lottie and Jo Jo revived Mommom she told them what she had seen. Finally, they all went to bed and forgot about the incident. The windows rattled and the doors squeaked all night, but they thought it was the wind making the noise.

The next morning they looked around the house but did not find any footprints. That night Mommom, Aunt Lottie and Jo Jo saw the face at the window again. They grabbed a light and ran outside to see who or what it was but could not find anything or anyone. The next day they took rakes and brooms and raked and swept the ground (there wasn't any grass) so that if anyone should come there would be tracks or prints. The face appeared again. The next morning they looked outside but there weren't any tracks at all. The face kept on appearing for a while. Then the family decided that Mommom should take the teeth back. Mommom took them back and buried them in the field.

After that the face didn't appear. Summer came and Mommom, Lottie and Jo Jo and the family would sit on the porch quite a bit. (The porch stretched across the front of the house.) One evening they saw a ball of fire dancing up the dogtrot, and the peculiar noises started again. Finally, one morning they went out and found that something or someone had moved the whole front porch away from the house. And there weren't any footprints. They moved out of the house immediately!

22 ☠

Mark's Mill, near Warren, was the scene of a battle during the Civil War. There is a story about a Confederate officer who got wounded in the face by an exploded artillery shell. A Confederate supply train had been attacked by the Yankees, and that was the cause of the battle. Now the officer knew which wagon was carrying the gold shipment, and somehow he managed to crawl back through the bushes to the wagon, although he was blinded. He set fire to the wagon so it would burn down around the gold to prevent the Yankees getting hold of it. The blind and wounded soldier was taken to a field hospital where he died, not knowing what became of the gold. It has been said that ever once in a while you can see the soldier's ghost walking blindly about the battlefield with his arms outstretched, looking for his gold.

Another story connected with Mark's Mill has to do with some dead Yankees. After the small battle was over, the Yankees had to get out fast. They didn't have time to bury their dead, and they knew the Confederates wouldn't bury them. So they dropped as many as they could down a well. People say that if you hear some moans and groans echoing around the vicinity it is the dead Yankees wanting out of the well.

23 ☠

In the eastern part of Johnson County, not far from the historic little stream of Roan's Creek, there is a large gap which extends some distance back into Doe Mountain known as Songo Hollow. This section is very heavily forested and thick with underbrush. People seldom pass through it, especially near nightfall for it is a haunted region and has been so since the Civil War.

On a little knoll in the wilderness there is a heap of stone, once a chimney, which marks the site of Samuel Songo's cabin. Little is known among the settlers, except for the fact that he was noted as a man of great physical strength. He immigrated to Johnson County from Kentucky and brought along with him a beautiful wife. But it was rumored throughout the settlement that Songo belonged to the hostile party of a feud that was brewing, and early one morning as he was leaving his cabin, he was shot by an enemy in ambush. No one knew who killed him, and they had not known him long enough to care.

Two hunters passing the road that was then the stagecoach route to North Carolina heard a woman scream, and when they made their way to the cabin, they found that Mrs. Songo had stabbed herself with her husband's hunting knife and was lying in the doorway. The neighbors came and buried them near their home. But no one cared to live in the cabin where the strange couple had spent so short a time, for their rest was sure to be disturbed by the weird screams of the pretty wife of Samuel Songo as she grieved over the death of her husband and killed herself in despair.

24 ☠

During the War between the States, when the Potter–Stanfield feud was raging in the upper part of Johnson County, the Bloody Third rang with rifle shots from the skirmishes of the guns in battle, and the members of the victorious parties brought their prisoners across the hills. These victims were tortured, imprisoned or killed outright.

In the torturing process, the cave, called the Jingling Hole, played a most unique part. Since this cave has a straight descent of ninety feet, the victorious party—whether Potter or Stanfield—often placed an iron rod across the entrance. To this rod the culprit was forced to swing by his hands while his gloating captor tapped on his knuckles with the breech of his rifle, first on one hand and then on the other in rapid succession, causing an active display of gymnastics as the prisoner swung from hand to hand. Usually these victims were able to stand this torture and were released with bruised and blistered hands, to be preserved for future adventures; again, there was a casualty, as the victim rolled into the lake at the bottom of the cave.

The neighbors say that at night when they go 'possum hunting in the fall, they hear strange noises around the Jingling Hole. If they listen carefully they hear moans and groans, especially if the wind is blowing, and there is also the hollow sound of a gun breech cracking on knuckles, for the spirits of the Potters and Stanfields are not at rest but must still be torturing their victims.

25 ☠

The biggest story I ever heard was that during the Civil War an old fellow named Jack Walker lived up the river there on *this* side. And you know they had livestock back then at open range here, and the old feller was over there huntin' hogs when he had a nigger slave run away from him. A fellow, Bone, over there was runnin' the mill and the nigger slave run away from him and went over there and Bone was a'coverin' him up. And this old feller Jack Walker went over there and found him or somethin', got in contact with Bone some way, and Bone killed him. Buried him in the mud but didn't kill him dead, and he left old man Walker's one hand out of the mud, they found him that way.

And there wasn't any courts then, during the war. They impounded a jury and tried him, public trial, and they found him guilty. And hung him over there at the lake. And one of my great-aunts—I think it was a great-aunt—spun the rope that they hung him with…

But he and old man Walker had a run-in some way about the nigger, and he killed old man Walker. He was a—Bone was—a Yankee sympathizer.

And they was an old mill house there, but that mill sinking into that lake, I've never knowed that to be a fact. I've never heard what went with that old mill house, but they *said* that it was standing there when Bone was hung. And I've been told that that water rises and falls, you know. And there's a deep end of that lake where there ain't no bottom to it. They've never been able to find the bottom to it. And that lake, sometime it'll fill up full, and sometime it'll go down to a lower level. And they said right after Bone was hung that water rose up in that pond, up to the eave of that mill house.

26 ☠

It was day, and the river ran as it had always run, and then it was night, and with the next day there was a lake where the river had been. It was a large lake, and the river ran beside it. In between there was an island of farm about fifteen hundred acres in size, and it was to become very good farmland. A lake was born, and that is how the Indians told the white men it happened.

The lake was known as "the lake" for many years, for it was a lake without a name. The white man came, and they cleared the land and planted it in cotton. It was a plantation, and there were slave huts along the side of the lake. The people would fish in the lake, and they would go back and forth in boats to see their neighbors.

There was one old Negro who crossed the lake to see some people who lived on the other side, but he was never to return. The people sitting on their porch watched his small boat make its way back across the lake. They could see the light of the old man's lantern, but as he reached the middle it went away. They drug the lake all the next day, but they could never find him.

Some have said they have seen the old Negro with his lamp walking on the waters of the lake in the night. Many are scared of the lake, and they will not go near it in the darkness; many say that it is foolish, and the man does not walk on its waters. But today the lake is known by everyone as Spirit Lake.

27 ☠

One night at a party when things became dull, the conversation shifted aimlessly from one subject to another. In the course of this rambling conversation, a young man of the group teasingly belittled the bravery of women. The young ladies were immediately offended. They would prove that they were as brave as any man or group of men in the country. In fact, in order to prove their contention, a delegation of them would voluntarily go into the graveyard at the side of the hill without male escort.

But how would one know that they had really visited the graveyard and not merely hidden away until sufficient time had elapsed to make the young men think they had been there? They would solve that, too. They would carry forks and stick them upright in newly made graves, and these the young men could see the next morning. It was agreed, so the girls went.

The night was dark. A low-lying fog lay around the hills, and the trees dripped with moisture. The ghostly meetinghouse shining dimly nearby did not tend to add confidence to the hearts of the girls. The graveyard lay a good distance around the meetinghouse and up a hill.

When they reached the graveyard, there was hardly enough

courage left to take them in, but they took each other by the hand and thereby gained needed confidence. Finally, they were at the newly made graves. They stopped simultaneously and each embedded her fork to the hilt in the wet clay. Then they each arose—all except one! The awed girls who had risen had heard a slight shriek, and when they looked at their feet, there lay the white form of one of their companions. They fled. They thought a ghost had her.

The next morning the sun dispelled the fog enough to light up the stark face of the dead girl on the new-made grave. Some men pulled her up from the yellow mound. It was not a ghost that had her at all. It was the fork. In sticking it in the ground, she had caught her low-hanging skirt in the tines, and it had become fastened to the grave. She had died of heart failure.

28 ☠

One night Papa was coming from church. It was dark as pitch. Well, he walked along this old gravel road, and just before he got to the creek, near this old creek bed—and he had to cross the creek to get to the house—well, he heard something, like rock or gravel, you know, rolling, and he looked around and there was a man. He was just laying there on the ground and said he just lit up. He said the man got up and started walking up the creek bank and tried to get him to follow him. Why, it nearly scared him to death! He said he was never so afraid in his life. He said he heard something like someone stepping on a dead stick and looked away, and when he looked back, it was gone.

29a ☠

The courthouse is Carrollton, Alabama, is listed as, uh, one of the things in Alabama that's listed in *Ripley's Believe It or Not*. The reason it's listed is that a long time ago, there was supposed to be a hanging, a black man had murdered a white man for some unknown reason to me, and when the man claimed to be innocent—And they housed him in the jail in Carrollton. Carrollton is the county seat of Pickens County, the county I grew up in. And when they took the man up to the gallery in the court-house, the weather was real bad and they were going to hang him inside, and he told the sheriff and the others present that—that he was innocent and if they hung him that they would find out a white man had killed the man and that they would have hung an innocent man. So when they got ready to hang him an electrical storm came up and just as they hung the man this bolt of lightning struck the courthouse and the man's picture was transposed on the north gallery window.

And legend has it that this window has been removed a number of times and each time this face reappears on it. Now whether this is true or not I don't know, and of course, we that lived in Pickens County believed that they wouldn't take it out for anything, 'cause it's a little-bitty place and this is really its only claim to fame.

29b ☠

Eighty years ago, in Aliceville, Alabama, a man was arrested and tried for murder. All through the long trial the man pleaded innocence, but a verdict of guilty was handed down, and the judge sentenced him to be hung. After he was hung, it was discovered that the man had been innocent, and the real murderer was caught. Since that awful discovery, the image of a man's face has been outlined in the windowpane of the cell he stayed in throughout the trial. They have tried to wash it off but couldn't. A few years back, a rampant hailstorm knocked out or broke every window in the building except that one. Then they removed the pane and replaced it, but the image returned in the new one, and there it can still be seen.

30 ☠

Near the top of Stone Mountain in Johnson County, there is a large rock that juts out over a precipice known as Fiddler's Rock. It was here that Martin Stone charmed the rattlesnakes with his fiddle and met his untimely fate.

It seems that Martin Stone was noted as a fiddler. At dances, parties and all social gatherings, Martin and his fiddle were the center of attraction. Often on quiet Sundays in the summer, Martin sat on the big rock and played his fiddle. From their den underneath came the rattlesnakes, attracted by the music. They wriggled, danced and rattled, keeping time in a most uncanny manner. When Martin grew tired of playing, he often stopped and amused himself further by reaching for his shotgun and priding himself on the number that he could kill before they glided back into shelter.

But one day, as Martin played, he became fascinated with the wriggling, writhing mass below him. In and out twined the smooth golden bodies, reflecting the ever-changing lights and shadows. He forgot to reach for his gun, the bow dropped from his nerveless fingers, and slowly he felt himself sliding downward toward the snakes.

The next day, a neighbor found his lifeless body, in which had been buried the fangs of many rattlesnakes. Nearby lay the fragments of his broken fiddle. The neighbors buried him and mourned his loss. But ever since they have avoided Fiddler's Rock as a haunted place, for on summer evenings, when the wind is in the trees, the whine of Martin's fiddle may still be heard as he charms the rattlesnakes and, in his own fascination, forgets to reach for his gun.

31 ☠

Well, it seems it happened many a year ago; Mama knowed the woman that was married to that man. I don't know of his real name; they called him Lightnin' as a nickname, 'cause he moved about so slow. Well, I don't know for sure but that he took to drinkin' and then to beatin' on his wife. She was a real good person and says she loved her husband, so she never did nothin' to make him stop.

His drinkin', it got worse and worse, till one day he up and left. Well, nobody knowed where he got off to, but some say he drowned in the river 'cause he couldn't swim. Shortly after that, his wife, she took real sick. She said she had the high fever, but everybody knowed she was sick in the heart 'cause that man of hers, he was gone. I don't understand why she could worry herself sick over a man that drunk most of the time—even on

Sundays—and beat her up till she was black and blue and could hardly walk. But black womans—they's that way about their mans. Well, Lightnin', he never come back to her, and by and by she died. Some folks say it was out-and-out murder 'cause he was what drove her to that grave. But nobody done nothin' about that 'cause couldn't nobody prove it.

Then that man, he come home one day lookin' to see where his wife was gone. Nobody done told him she was dead most 'cause of him. He didn't believe it when he found out she was dead. He said somebody killed her or took her and hid her out from him. Everybody was real scared of him 'cause he was filled with all them evil demons from drinkin'. One day he went out to the graveyard—that one on the hill—and he found her grave. Nobody knows for sure, but some folks say he dug her up to see for hisself that nobody was lying to him. He found her body and bones and all and then killed himself. Some folks say he died from grief, but I think he drunk hisself to death.

And to this very day, you can hear him a'beatin' on her some nights and you can hear her screamin' and moanin' 'cause their souls they ain't rested. Don't nobody go by there at night if you can help it, for that man, he's liable to chop you up or something else real bad. And if you do has to walk by there, don't never dare look at the graves, but look straight ahead and walk on by real fast.

I remember one night when we was kids, we got real brave and decided to walk by there, and sure enough you could hear that poor old woman screamin' but you had to listen real close. We was scared half to death. I had the shakes for a week and plenty of nightmares too. I ain't never once gone by there again walkin' at night—and I don't let my kids neither.

Some people now say it ain't true, but it is, 'cause I heard it myself. It's just like some folks not believin' in the good Lord, but it's true too, 'cause I seen him once. But that's another story, and you know about that already anyhow. Well, that's the story.

32a 💀

Well, on a night it would be storming, everybody around in the community would gather at my Grandpa's house because he had a cellar and nobody else did. And some of the older people would tell us kids about, uh, that building that was across the road from my Grandpa's house. They would tell us kids that caskets were still stored in the loft of the old casketmaker's shop. It was a long time ago, before any of us were born, and the guy that made the caskets had been dead for a long time.

Well, like I said, we'd all be sitting up there on the porch and watching the storms, and sooner or later one of the older people start talking about—about the building and how it had once been a casketmaker's shop and the man-who-owned-it's name was Ashberry Sago. And his son Morris would be sitting up there, and he would come up on the porch and he would tell about what a good business he had because he was the only casketmaker around there at that time. These caskets were good—they look a lot like they do today—even though completely handmade down there in that shop. Well, the people around there didn't like him too much because he always looked at you as though he was mentally measuring you up for a casket and wondering how long you would make him wait before you died and give him your business.

No one knows exactly how he died or when, but the older people say that caskets are still stored in the loft of the old shop and that one is an unfinished casket for a child, and on stormy nights you can hear him hammering away on an unfinished casket for a child who has long been cold in her grave. It is commonly known that until recently his casket lay unoccupied because of his mysterious disappearance. However, only a short while ago the old shop was torn down.

32b ☠

Well, Ashberry—we called him Rip—made caskets for all the local townsfolk. He did this for over fifty years—actually more than that if you count his father. A doctor moved in one day, where Rayburn lives now, but was so scared—this was in 1924 or thereabouts—he moved out. Well, this old casketmaker seemed always his happiest when death was in the air. He would look you up and down when he saw you—made you feel kind of crazy. The oddest thing about this old man was that he made his own casket and prided himself on this fact and would even show people when they had a death in the family. Well, he had a call for a child's casket and set to work on it, but before it was ever finished he disappeared. The people believed he would always return. During the stormiest part of a storm you can hear him at work trying to finish out his work. I tell kids if they ain't good, he will build them a casket.

33 ☠

One night me and a friend of mine were walking by a graveyard at night. While we were passing the graveyard, we heard a noise coming from it. We then walked over into the graveyard to see what was making the noise. When we got into the graveyard, we saw a baby crying on one of the tombstones. My friend picked the baby up, and then we started down the road toward his home.

As we walked down the road, he noticed that the baby got heavier and heavier. He then looked at it and saw that it had turned into an old man with a gray beard. He tried to put him down, but he couldn't. The old man told him that he would never be able to do it until he took him back to the place where he found him. He took him back and left him there. The baby was a ghost!

34 ☠

I remember when I was about eight years old, one night I was walking home from the theater. I only lived a few blocks away. It was about eleven. I saw a horse in the far end of the city grave-yard. The horse was bending down over a grave and pawing. When he saw me, he ran away. It struck me as sort of strange to see a horse in the graveyard.

The next morning I told my granny about the horse. She told me this legend about a man who'd been a soldier in World War I. He was in the cavalry, and he was a bugler. He died a long time before the night I saw that horse, and he is buried in the cemetery. Granny told me that a lot of people had seen that horse and heard the bugler in the cemetery. The people said during a full moon is when you can hear the bugle and see the horse at the grave. I saw the horse, but I didn't hear the bugle.

35 ☠

I live just over that little ridge, I've lived there ten years. We built a little house there. There was the most impossible, impossible, unbelievable things that could have ever happened at that place. It was when you least expected anything that it happened. The first thing we ever noticed was one night, there was a light over our house, a big light like the sun was shining right there, and it was real dark. My husband first noticed it and he called me out there. It came over the spring—we had a spring out there and a tree by it—and you could have counted ever limb on that tree. Well, we stood there and watched that until we got too tired and went to bed.

Then, the next thing, one night—the moon shined that night—we walked out in the yard and was standing there looking around. Over in the field where we had cows and horses out, we heard this horse coming. It sounded just like a man coming up the road, and then all of a sudden it stopped—the sound. And there was not nothing. My husband said that beat any damn thing he'd seen.

Then one night he was gone and the children had done gone to bed. Now my oldest stepdaughter wasn't asleep. I was just settin' there a'readin' and I heard the kitchen door latch rattle, and I thought it was the dog a'bumpin' the door with its nose. Well, then the front door latch started rattlin'. It was just an old house we built ourselves, it had these big old hinge doors, and when you'd open them the hinges would squeak. Well, these doors started *scree-ak-ing*, like sombody was opening them easy, you know. Well, I raised up my head and my stepdaughter raised up her head on her elbow. It went back to *scree-ak-ing* back about halfway, and then it stopped. And that door didn't no more move than that door's moving now. Both of us just sat there and looked at it, there wasn't nothing we could do. You talk about a creepy feeling.

Then one evening the children went to the spring to get some water; it was the fall of the year and the leaves were dead. They said, "Mama, something fell out of this tree out here and we can't find it and it's making the awfullest racket you ever heard." And I went, and the leaves was laying there, they wasn't stirring, but it went like a dog having a fit or dying or something out there in them leaves. Well, I thought that maybe there was something in under the leaves, and I took me a stick, and I raked and I raked. There wasn't nothing under there, there wasn't even a board

OTHER HAUNTED PLACES   67

under there. And then when I quit, it started again.

It was just everything. Sometimes I'd take my kids and go to the store, and I'd look back and I'd wish that everybody was out of them mountains and wouldn't have to go back no more.

36 💀

I went to school, college, in Arkadelphia at Henderson State Teachers College, Henderson State College now. OBU (Ouachita Baptist University) is in the same town, right across the street from Henderson, and so they are great rivals. When I was going to college there, this was a tradition as well as a legend.

Back when Henderson first became a college it was called Henderson Brown College, and it was a Methodist school. One year a boy from Henderson fell in love with a girl from OBU. Their friends tried to break them up because they were from different schools and different religions. Finally they succeeded in getting them apart, and while they were dating other people the boy fell in love with someone else. The girl from OBU was upset about this, and she tried to get her lover back, but there was nothing she could do, so she committed suicide during homecoming week.

Every year during homecoming week the ghost of the girl from OBU—she is called the Black Lady—comes back through the girls' dorms at Henderson looking for the girl who stole her lover. Every year during homecoming week the junior and senior girls at Henderson get together and go through the freshmen dorms and scare the girls. The freshmen have heard the story of the Black Lady, so they know what is happening.

37 💀

One time, it was late at night, I was working at night school with Mr. Carlisle. It was registration night, and we had collected a lot of money, and he said he was going to leave me in Room 521, which is way down the hall, to go to the guidance office to turn on the alarm. I said, "You are not going to leave me here alone with all of this money." At the time, I did not know anything about the ghost.

He said, "Well, come on and walk down there with me." While we were walking, just before we got to the cutoff down here, he says, "When we get to the 300 hall I want you to look and tell me what you see."

When we got down there, I looked and I said, "What in the hell is that?"

He said, "That's the ghost," and I took off. He was outlined in white; he was a real tall man. He was standing in the middle of the hall. We have breezeways, and it looked like that was where he was standing, and that was why I saw him, because of the light reflection. I never believed in ghosts. I did see him; he was standing there with his hands on his hips. He was not doing anything; he was just standing there with his hands on his hips. I could tell he had on a skinny tie. It was a real thin tie; he had on a suit and a white shirt; that was why the tie showed up. That is all I saw. I left, and Mr. Carlisle had to find me. I was scared to death. Mr. Carlisle explained to me that it was Mr. Pair. He said that Mr. Pair is seen a lot, especially at night.

From that time on, I started hearing a lot of stories. It seems like they used to have a problem with the alarm going off for no apparent reason. You often heard it said that Mr. Pair had scared away anything that might happen to Airport (High School). It's strange because nothing has ever happened to the old part of the school. He has never been seen in the new parts, and they have been broken into. Nobody has ever broken into the old part. Mr. Rivers says that he will not hurt you; he may make you hurt yourself, but he will not hurt you.

3 Headless and Screaming Ghosts and Revenants

Perhaps because of the popularity of Washington Irving's **Legend of Sleepy Hollow,** ghosts are frequently thought of as headless figures on horseback. Certainly, a strong folk tradition—derived primarily from England—of headless ghosts on horseback does exist. Headless ghosts, however, are more often found walking, sometimes carrying their head under their arms. On other occasions the headless figure is standing at a certain spot and jumps up behind the rider as the horse passes by.

In the following tales, the actions of various headless Southern ghosts are related, some of them having only a small portion of body visible. Also recounted here are the activities of some invisible "returners" from the dead, or **revenants.** As these texts demonstrate, the headless ghosts and revenants often appear for a specific reason, perhaps as an omen of impending death or to avenge an injury.

My grandfather used to tell me when I was a little girl about one of his sons which he used to live with. He said his son had a good wife and two children, but his wife wasn't strong and had to lie in bed most all the time. My uncle wasn't good to her because she couldn't work. She loved him, but he would only curse her when she tried to tell him.

Years passed on, but matters grew worse instead of better. My uncle fell in love with a Negro woman, and he began going to see her. Every night he would leave his sick wife at home and go to see the Negro woman. One night his wife prayed and asked him to stay with her, but he would not listen to her. He went on to see the Negro woman.

Then, about nine o'clock, he started back home. As he went up the hill a small man stepped in front of him. He spoke, but the little man didn't answer. My uncle began to shoot at him but couldn't hit him. Then he started to run. Just then, the little man jumped on his back and put two woolly paws around his neck. This thing stayed on his back, and every step he took, it seemed to get heavier. He carried it for about three miles up the mountain before he came to the house. Just as he got to the steps, the little man jumped off and ran.

The little man came again the next night to the big farmhouse and kept him awake all night. He would come every night and walk through the hall and up the stairs. The doors would not stay shut, and the windows would rattle. The little man could not be seen, but he could be heard. One night, grandfather sprinkled flour on the stairs to see if any tracks could be seen next morning. But next morning they couldn't see any tracks. They would even bar the stair door, but it would come open. This never left until this sinful man fell on his knees and began to pray. After that he was never bothered any more, for he became a religious man.

39 ☠

The way this happened, I was comin' along the road up there on the Markland Hill and thought I was overtakin' Oscar Tipton. I did walk up a little fast. Wanted to see him. And I was gainin' on him. Then when he got about to the bars there on top of the hill, he turned in. Well, I kep' a'goin' it and when I got up there an' looked in at him I see that he had no head. And then I shore straightened out them roads. A little while atter that, eight or ten days I reckon, they brought Butler home dead. Butler was Aunt Frances' boy. Died of measles and double menthole, in the Army. I don't know what that double menthole is, but that's what they called it. Now it looked to me like that was a warnin' or somethin'.

40 ☠

Well, I'll tell you something: me and my dad, back when I was a boy, we'd wagon from—you know that was the only source of getting groceries—Ramsey, Virginia, out there through Norton, and we'd drove our wagons down. We had covered wagons loaded down with meal, flour, lard, coffee—you know, we'd get all the groceries and bring 'em back. And so we couldn't make it with the horses and all in one day's time, you know, leaving out of the Kentucky River there and going over to Norton. We'd have to, you know, camp out at night.

So we's up there, and we got out and it was a'blowin' snow; it was in November, and we got out and we got our firewood, you know. We kept our bedrolls with us all the time, and a lot of times if it was real bad, why, we'd manage some way to crawl in the wagon, but if it was real good weather we'd just build a fire—we always kept plenty of firewood, and we had our bedroll to keep us warm. We'd do our own cookin'—cookin' on a campfire.

We had a boy with us…about seventeen, eighteen years old, and he was tellin' an awful big lie. He kept on saying, "Who's that man goin' yonder with no head on? Who's that man goin' yonder with no head on?" Finally I looked up. I wasn't payin' no mind to him 'cause you couldn't believe anything he said. My dad, he didn't believe in anything like that at all, and I looked up and seen it myself. Yeah, I really looked up and seen it. And so, uh, I woke my dad up. And he said, "Has he learnt you to start lying, too?"

And I said, "No." We called him Pap, you know, that's the old way, the mountain way, Pa or Pap or Pappy or something like that.

And I said, "No, Pap, sure as we're here I seen it." I said, "Watch now for yourself, and don't say you didn't see it, 'cause I seen it four or five times crossin' that road."

And he looked, and that was the worst surprised man, when he seen that, that I ever seen in my life. And he said, "I'd have never believed anything like that in my life. But that's really happened." And the old man, he never went to sleep anymore that night. He set there and kept a good fire—good and warm—said, "Now I believe you."

It looked like a man, and he was a well-dressed man. Looked like he had on a real fresh-pressed serge suit, and, uh, it looked like you could have seen his head stickin' up, but he had no head on *whatsoever.* You could see his neck stickin' up—he had a long neck. He went across there—you'd never see him come back across, he was always going that same way every time.

---

41 ☠

The most famous of the Sewanee ghosts is the headless gownsman. The legend goes that in years gone by, some time in the past, there was a group of theologues, or seminary students, cramming for mid-semester exams. It was late into the night, and one of the students, being particularly diligent or particularly guilty, whichever the case may be, wanted to study considerably later than his roommates. An argument and a scuffle ensued, and the candle the student was studying by went out. When the fellow reached over to find the candle his head fell off, the theory being that the poor theologue had crammed his head so full of information that it just spun right off.

Now the headless gownsman was supposed to have been seen by a lady named Mrs. Tucker or Rucker or somesuch. It seems Mrs. Tucker was returning late one night from Forensic Hall. She was returning home and met a figure whom she assumed to be a student, since he had a gown, and Sewanee students do wear gowns, those who have been inducted into the Order of Gownsmen. Anyway, they wear their gowns to class, indeed, anytime they leave their rooms except to go to sporting events or to work or such things.

At any rate, Mrs. Tucker met this gowned figure and assumed it to be a student and expected it to greet her as she met it. But it didn't happen; the gowned figure kept getting closer and closer to her. It made no effort to get out of her way; it didn't speak to her. As it brushed by, she turned around and it was gone. She also said that she thought she saw a face on it but couldn't recognize it as anyone she had ever seen.

Now this wouldn't be too unusual on most university campuses, that is to say, someone not recognizing a given student. But this is exceptionally rare at a place such as Sewanee. The student body of the university itself being limited to something like six hundred students and Sewanee being a relatively isolated community, everyone pretty well gets to recognize the faces of everybody else.

At any rate, ever since Mrs. Tucker's experience people have reportedly seen the headless gownsman. Now usually, the reports come from someone who saw someone who talked to someone who knew someone who saw the headless gownsman. It's still alleged that the head of this gownsman that fell off from having too much knowledge crammed into it remained in Wyndcliff Hall. Now, Wyndcliff Hall don't no longer exist. When the theologues moved out it was torn down, and the theologues moved into what is now known as St. Luke's Hall.

In those days, the days when the legend of the headless gownsman originated, all the seminary students were single, or the large majority of them were single, and in St. Luke's Hall the single seminarians live on the fourth floor, which is up above the classrooms and the library. Now the head of this gownsman, as I say, is to have remained in Wyndcliff Hall. But when they tore Wyndcliff Hall down and the theologues moved into St. Luke's Hall, the head of this gownsman moved in there.

It is said to be ominously present during times of exams, especially mid-terms and finals. Each year someone claims to have some sort of scuffle with the ghost or sees the ghost in his room. It is said to come down the stairs and then count the stairs as it comes down, always the right number of bumps per the number of steps it comes down. Normally, it only shows up during the exam period. Now this is the head of the headless gownsman.

There is at least one sighting per year of the headless gownsman. Again, most reports come from someone who saw someone who talked to somebody who heard somebody say they had seen him.

42 ☠

This is the truth. I was a little boy around about six or seven years old. We were down the street picking berries at night. We had two flashlights and we seen something come out the bushes, and it was real black and had white hands and it was beckoning for me and my sister and brother. All of us, we took off running. I like to dropped my berries, but I helt onto 'em. This haint, he ran by so fast, we thought it was something like a rocket or something. It was moving kind of fast, and my daddy seen it when he was back there on the back porch. He looked back and said, "Dere dat haint go. Dere he go."

And he went so fast that he was zooming down the road—they got a dog pound back there now—and I don't believe we've seen another one since that one. It did not have no head. His head was cut off. He was real black, and he had nothing but white hands. His hands was so white they looked silver. You couldn't see nothing but his hands during the night, beckoning for us, but we never did come where he was. He said he might git us the next time.

43 ☠

Out at Abraham Baldwin Agricultural College, you know, enterin' freshmen hear all kinds of garbage, you know, people tellin' you stories. And one of the first ones I ever heard was about the Omega Road overpass—75, just south of Tifton. There's a story that a girl used to go here from Florida. No tellin' how many years ago. The time period is indefinite. Could have been ten, fifteen years ago.

She had to stay late for some reason. She wanted to go home that weekend. Instead of leavin' back down there she had somethin' to do and didn't get to leave until that night. You know, she was in a hurry, and leavin' right there under that overpass she had a wreck. Now it's unclear as to whether or not it was a two-car collision or if she just wrecked or what happened, what the cause was.

But the spooky part about it is, it's said that you can go out here right headin' south, on the way to Valdosta, and right after you go under that overpass you'll hear the sound of tires squallin'...and you can hear it two or three different times. Different pitches of tires, tires squallin'.

44 ☠

One night we come up here to Old Man Sipes, lived over there in the Brown house. I'd been over there to see him about some hay, and I went on 'cross that bridge and on down the road. Earl had the cows—he was just a little feller—and I went up to the house to see about the hay while Earl was drivin' the cows.

Went on down the road, and I looked down beside of me and there 'as a dog walkin', just trottin' along. He just trotted on alongside of me. And he was a big black-lookin' dog—big dark dog. That dog stood up that tall, but he just trotted along like he was one of those big police dogs. You've seen those big dark police dogs. He was big as one of those big police dogs, and he just trotted right alongside of me.

I was smaller than I am now. I didn't weigh but 'bout a hundred and twenty-five. Looked like to me my breath was comin' and goin', and that dog just trottin' on alongside of me. He never barked. He never made no noise. He just trotted right alongside of me just like he'd a'been my pet dog.

And when he got there to Mr. Blake's gate, he just walked right around in front of me, and I just slowed down when he walked round in front of me; he went right through that gate crack, and that dog disappeared. And I ain't never seen that dog from that day to this, and I'm tellin' you, man, I never did look fer him. Naw sir, that 'as the biggest dog I'd seen in this country, and I ain't never seen that dog no more, but that dog disappeared; when he went through that gate that dog just disappeared right in the air. Never did see him. Never did see whichaway he went nor nothing, but I heerd the chain and heerd the gate rattle and I saw him when he went through and when he got on the other side, but soon as you turn your eyes it's gone.

Talk 'bout steppin', I didn't come back up this road no more after dark. When I got home I told Earl, I said, "I seen a ghost tonight."

He said, "Where'd you see him, Mama?"

I said, "Right up there. Right down below the old Brown bridge." And I said, "He walked right side of me till I got to Mr.

Blake's gate, and he just went right through that crack. When he went through that crack I could hear that gate shakin' and the chain, and when I looked that dog were gone."

Didn't see no more dog. I quit comin' up this road after dark by myself.

45 ☠

I was comin' down these bridges at Coal Run one time, and if the river was up or anything you had to walk the railroad. So I went to the show uptown and it was about twelve o'clock (midnight), and there come a big storm. You know where Cedar Creek is, don't you, that cut in Cedar Creek? Well, I saw two eyes a'comin', looked like they was about that far (a few inches) apart. Every time it would lightning I couldn't see those eyes, but when it was dark I could see those eyes a'comin'. I didn't know what to do, so I got off on the ground, up on the tracks, and I got me two big rocks and I throwed them at it and I didn't dent it nor nothin'. Just went on through it. I didn't have no light atall, that's all there was. No, it wasn't no train. It was something in the middle of the tracks. You couldn't hear it. All I could see was just them eyes. After it got past me, I didn't see it. It went on by me; I got off the tracks onto the ground. That's the worst scared I've ever been in my life. I was about eighteen years old.

4 Ghosts and Hidden Treasure

One of the most popular reasons for American ghosts to return is to reveal the whereabouts of hidden treasure. The theme is ancient, being first reported in a Buddhist myth but coming to this country primarily by way of the British Isles, where it is still a very strong tradition. Frequently reported from England, Wales and Ireland—although rarely from Scotland—the idea of a ghost returning to aid humans in finding hidden treasure has remained popular in the United States since Colonial times. Usually, it is a male ghost that returns, but there are many reports of female specters. Sometimes the ghost returns as a dismembered corpse, but frequently it takes no human form. The ghost may return as a dog or some other animal or as an object or a phantom ship. Sometimes it is a ghost light that points out the treasure, at other times merely a noise. In most instances, the ghost disappears, never to return again once the treasure is found.

Accounts of ghosts and hidden treasure are contained in the several texts that follow. In most respects the Southern apparitions discussed here are typical of those generally found in American tradition.

Not far from Mountain City, in a section called "The Bloody Third," stand the ruins of an old stone house around which hangs a peculiar legend of "the haint that couldn't be fathomed." The house remained vacant for some years after the Civil War, until Dr. Houston, a promising young physician with a brilliant mind and an unfortunate taste for drink, bought it, settled there and took up the surrounding mountain practice.

A short time after moving into this house, the members of the Houston family were often disturbed by queer noises. Early in the evening came a decided patter of feet on the floor. With three distinct knocks on the door, this invisible guest would enter. Then came the patter of feet on the broad oak stair as it made its round of the room above returning by the same route, back to the large fireplace in the broad living room, after which it took its departure, giving three farewell knocks.

Mrs. Houston, being a woman of strong character, was not afraid of the ghost, but she was curious to know its origin, so she sprinkled flour thickly over the stairsteps, hoping to get an imprint of the airy foot. She then listened to the pat on the stairs, but no track was ever made. All was smooth whiteness. She grew to know when to expect it and accepted it calmly. But if the doctor happened to be at home when the tapping occurred, he was much disgruntled and would often follow it upstairs and back, mumbling as he came.

As the neighbors became more wrought up and curious in regard to this strange apparition, several reliable men of the vicinity gathered and decided they would investigate the situation. They made pallets on the floor in the hall and arranged to sleep in front of the door so as to intercept the footsteps, but their sleep was not satisfactory. A sudden gust of warm air settled heavily on their chests, and they were nearly suffocated, being held down in meek submission while the footsteps passed over them. The men rose quietly the next morning and left. They were never known to mention the subject to their friends, and when questioned in regard to it they briefly told their experience, making no pretense of understanding it.

One evening Dr. Houston came in drunk. He sat with the pistol cocked, waiting for the ghost. As the three knocks sounded on the door he bounded forward to meet it and followed it up the stairs shooting and cursing volubly. The footsteps were not disturbed by the doctor's violence. They made their rounds with regular tread. As three farewell knocks sounded, Dr. Houston emptied his pistol into the outside darkness several times and closed the door.

Strange to say, this visitor never returned, but years afterwards, when the huge fireplace was torn away, a skeleton was found underneath the hearthstone, and fastened to the ledge of rock was a huge roll of Confederate bills. It was thought that the unfortunate victim had been killed for his money, which was fastened to the ledge for safekeeping, but the murderer was killed before he could return for his booty.

47 🕱

There was an old house down around Snow Hill that people said was haunted. Things had been seen there and things heard, and the man that owned the place said that anybody who could stay there all night could have it. There was a Mr. Jones who decided to give it a try, and he took his family with him to spend the night. Late that night, after the children had been put to bed, Mr. Jones and his wife were sitting by the fire reading the Bible, when a black cat came down the stairs and passed through the room and went out the door. Mr. Jones went on reading the Bible, and a while later, a man in a black overcoat came down the stairs and disappeared. Mr. Jones kept on reading the Bible. Later on, the same man in the same black overcoat came back down the stairs, and Mr. Jones asked him, "What in the name of the Father, the Son and the Holy Ghost do you want?" The man in the black overcoat then told him to go upstairs. He told him where there was a part of a room that had been sealed off and that inside it he would find a black overcoat with some money in the pocket. Mr. Jones went upstairs and found the money. The overcoat was the same as the one the ghost had been wearing.

48 ☠

Now I don't know if it's true or not, but she told it to be true. She was out chopping cotton. This was after she got married and moved down around Hugo. Her baby was sick, and every now and then she'd go back to the house to see about him. Once, when she was walking back to the house, she saw a woman coming towards her down the path. And then the woman disappeared. Well, Mrs. Tillman had to keep going back and forth from the field to the house, and the same thing happened twice more. The third time she asked the woman, "What in the name of the Father, the Son and the Holy Ghost do you want?" Nearby there stood an old walnut tree beside a graveyard, and the woman told Mrs. Tillman to step off ever so many steps from that tree toward the graveyard and dig and she'd find some money. She did, and she said she found some. Like I said, I don't know if it's true or not, but she told it to be true.

49 ☠

My daddy told me this when I was a little boy. It happened when they were living on this man's farm in one of the old houses. And, you see, most of the land around there had been owned by the McCormicks—they were the rich people back in them days. And they say the last two sisters died. But they buried some enchanted money before they died. And they said what made them think that it was some money at the house—say because they be all the time hearing things and get them feeling like people get when they meet a ghost or something.

Well, they—Daddy and some more fellows around in there— they decided to try and dig that money. So they all got together with their bits of knowledge and everything. So they all decided to make a ring using cups and saucers that were filled with salt and surround the place where the money was. You see, the evil spirit couldn't cross over that ring. They did this. Then they had a man to get on each corner of the house to watch, because the money was right under the edge of the house. After the men got to every corner of the house, they started digging.

After a while, he said they heard something coming through the cotton field. And they looked up. He say there was something that looked like a great big hog coming down through there! It was coming right at them, so they ran into the house. He said that after they got into the house, that thing ran under it and just shook that whole house like a tornado had hit it! So that scared them off, and they didn't try to dig that money no more.

Somehow the word got out to those professional guys out of McColl, South Carolina. So when they came up there, they brought a man that could talk to spirits. This man brought a Bible and some whiskey with him. He said that if the spirits that were guarding the treasure were drunkards, he could get them to come to him with the whiskey; if they were religious, he could get them to come with the Bible.

So this man walked down to the edge of the woods to contact and ask the spirits for the money. After the man got down to the woods, Daddy said that they saw the two old women that had died. When the man offered them the whiskey, they would not come. Then he offered them the Bible. One then came close enough to him so that he could talk to her. He asked her for the money, and she finally agreed to let them dig the money. And they got the money!

50 🕱

I remember one night before the fireplace, there was my uncle—my father's brother—tellin' not only me as a child, but my father, about this occurrence across the mountain. As I say, many folks from this side of the mountain went over in season to work for the big farmers in the valley. These mountain people used to go over into the valley in the fall of the year at harvest time in late summer to harvest the wheat. They'd go back in autumn to harvest the corn crops. Everything was done by hand in those days, that is, as far as cuttin' corn. And then after the corn was in, they would cut wood for the winter for these big farmers over there.

And so as my uncle related, he had started out—in those days you didn't work by the clock, you worked by the sun—he started out just before daylight so he could get to his work. He had started that mornin' up the hollow, up to the woods, a hollow called Lewis's Run. Most hollows had a stream in 'em; a stream was a run. And he said it was a dreary lookin', spooky lookin' place.

And he said the farther he got, the worse he felt. He felt cold chills. And he said he looked up the hollow and he saw a woman in old-time attire like his mother used to wear. And he said he didn't think anyone lived up there, so he asked himself, "Well, why would a woman be way up in this mountain this early in the mornin', a wild-lookin' place like this."

He said he kept walkin' and she kept comin'. And said when she got near him the clothes in particular didn't look natural, and he noticed she never batted an eye, she never blinked an eye just like she was lookin' through him and walked right by him and said he felt a chill and turned around. There was nobody there. And he said he went on up until he got to a good place to cut the wood and said the more he worked, the more apprehension he felt about being up there, and he started out. And said when he got back to the self-same spot that he had met this woman comin' down, he saw her comin' back again. And he said his heart stood still then. And he had always heard, if you were confronted with anything supernatural or anyone from the grave, to ask them in the name of the Lord what they wanted.

And he said when she got up in front of him that time, she didn't attempt to pass. She stopped right in front of him. And said it just paralyzed him, ev'rything but his tongue, and he said he did manage to get out, "What in the name of the Lord do you want?" And he said she pointed to a cliff on another mountain and said, "You see those rocks over there?" She said, "For one hundred years my bones been layin' in a cave under those rocks." Said, "I was murdered one hundred years ago, and my body was hid there, and if you will go git my bones and give 'em a Christian burial," said, "you'll be greatly rewarded for it." And said she just disappeared.

He come out and he told these people in the community what he thought he saw, and he tried to get someone to go with him, and they laughed him to scorn. Naturally, the experience he'd had the first time had unnerved him enough he wasn't goin' to take a chance of meetin' her again in a remote place, so he didn't go. But I heard him swear in my father's house that that was absolutely true. That's how I heard it; he was tellin' my father.

51 ☠

There was once a house that had a room where no bed could be kept in a certain corner. This was called Old Sutton's corner. A family lived there, and the husband's mother lived with them. Now this corner where no bed could be kept was a very desirable place since it was in the corner by the fireplace. Every time a bed was placed in this corner it would jump out in the middle of the floor.

Well, one night, just as the family was fixing to go over to a neighbor's to stay till bedtime, Granny, as she was called, said that she was going to have her bed in that corner. The son told her that Old Sutton would get her, too. She said that her bed was going in that corner, Sutton or no Sutton.

The family went on, and it was late bedtime when they started back home. After they crossed a little ridge and got to where they could see the house, it was full of fire, the blazes of light shooting out at the windows. All the family started running toward the house, very scared as to what might have happened to Granny. When they got through the yard gate, all the fire and light went out of the house. They went in the house, and there set Granny's bed out in the middle of the floor with her looking scared. She was not hurt at all, but she never did try to put a bed in that corner again.

Years later, when the house was torn down, a roll of money was found hidden in the walls of the house near the corner where nobody could get a bed to stay. And that was the last of Old Sutton and his troubles.

52 ☠

My wife's brother and his family bought a place and moved into the house that was on it. There had been some talk that nobody had been able to live at this place, but they never thought much about that, just thought it was some scary tale people had got in their head and started telling. They moved on in anyway.

There was a big rock fireplace in the big house, but they didn't sleep in this room; they slept in the back room. Well, it hadn't been long after they moved till they began hearing noises at night—just like the big rocks might be jumping out of the chimney and bouncing around over the floor. When they'd go in the room, everything would stop and there'd be no more noise, but as soon as they'd go back to bed it would start all over again. Finally, Henry's wife said she couldn't stand it any longer, and so they just sold out and left.

Well, the feller they sold to had the same trouble, so he just tore down the house to build another. When the old chimney and fireplace was torn down, they found a jar of gold pieces hidden right above the jambs. When the new house was put up, there was no more noises or trouble of any kind. It was all because of the hidden money.

53

My grandpa lived on this hill place, and Great-Grandpa lived down there at the well. One night Papa wanted to go to church. Grandma and her sister, Bertha, didn't want him to go. They said, "Don't go off and leave us."

Grandpa said, "There ain't nothing going to hurt you, and they ain't nothing for you to be afraid of." Grandpa said, "I'll have my gun."

Well, he went on down there to church and started back. Well, there's a white oak tree down the road that stood on the right. Well, he got up there even with the tree, and there were those two graves on the upper side of the road. Well, this woman came out from behind the tree and started running toward Papa. Well, Papa just stopped. He said she had big brown eyes and long brown hair and was just standing there looking right at Papa. And he said he could see her bat her eyes and the moon was shining as bright as day.

He said he just stood there looking at her and never said a word. And he heard a noise and turned his head, and when he looked back she had disappeared. Well, Papa told some of the older people what he had saw and all, and they said, "If you had said, 'Lord have mercy, what do you want?' she would have told you." What folks told Papa was that her husband was buried there, and there was money buried with him.

5 Traveling Ghosts

Most ghosts are bound to a single place, but there are those who carry their haunting farther afield. Usually the wraiths move about by horseback or automobile, rather than by supernatural means. This activity has a lengthy and somewhat elderly tradition, being found throughout Russia and much of Europe. It is documented that as early as the 1660s, people were telling stories about these traveling ghosts, and they were undoubtedly being discussed prior to that time.

Some such tales involve a dead lover who returns and carries his sweetheart behind him on horseback. His goal is to carry her with him into the grave; in most versions he succeeds, but in a few, the girl is rescued at the last moment. Perhaps the best known European legend concerning a wandering ghost is that of the Flying Dutchman. In this story, a sea captain, because of his wickedness, is doomed to eternally sail his phantom ship without coming into harbor. "The Flying Dutchman" is the exception to the rule that the traveling ghosts do not cover distances of more than a few miles.

In the texts that follow, we will encounter some ghosts traveling in the South. Included among them is "The Vanishing Hitchhiker," a ghost tale that differs from most of the others in this section in that the ghost is a woman.

54

My grandfather, W.T. Dollar, he was a drummer, a horseback drummer for R.J. Reynolds Tobacco Company of Winston-Salem, and he drummed tobacco, you know, sold snuff and chewing tobacco. And the first thing, he always rode up by White Top through Konnarock when he was heading home, and he would always have to ride by the Devil's Stairs at sundown, and something got on the horse behind him, you know, and his horse started fretting, and he couldn't control it. His horse got kind of out of control with him.

And there's a church still standing, known as the Oak Grove Baptist Church now. When he come by there—when he got to the church—the horse just came to a complete stop without his controlling it, and when it did, why, it was just something getting off his horse, and he rode on in, which he lived about, oh, three quarters of a mile up the road at the homeplace. It's burned down now, you know. It was behind Paul Elliott's garage where an old junkpile is now.

He said when he got home, there was something, something on his horse. It looked like white marks of some kind, something you might say looked like chalk marks or something in the shape of somebody's legs or something—like somebody's legs on his horse's flanks, you know. He wiped to see if it was sweat from where the horse was a'frettin', but it wasn't, he said; it wasn't sweat. It was white marks like somebody had gotten on there with something on behind the saddle there. Whatever it was, wasn't on the saddle there; it was on behind the saddle. Ever what it was, sitting there behind him, had hung down and touched the horse's flanks, and my grandfather at that time, as anyone could witness, kept the best horse, 'cause he depended on his horse for his livelihood.

Now from that day on, it was always told to me, you could never get my grandfather to pass the Devil's Stairs at night. If he was caught below there, he'd always spend the night with Dr. Minnie Blevins, who lived in a house which is still standing there just below the road there in that real stiff curve.

55a 💀

A long time ago, an Indian couple was to be married, another ordinary marriage, as it may appear. But as time went on, the economic status of the family went from fair to very poor. When the couple had its first baby, a boy, the father knew he couldn't feed him, so after thinking about what was best for the child, he went to the river, and after asking God for forgiveness he dropped the child in the river. The husband believed he was doing the right thing and repeated his feat as each child was born. Each time, the townspeople heard the wife screaming, *"Ay, mi hijo (Oh, my son)"* in an eerie tone.

When her last son was born, she was determined to let him live. She went down to the river, and after her husband dropped the boy, she went after him. Since she wasn't skilled in the art of swimming, she drowned along with her son.

Nobody thought much of it after her death, but one foggy night, one of the farm workers saw the ghostly figure of a woman and child in the river. The woman screamed in her high-pitched voice, "Oh, my son!" After that night, the ghost appeared on the water and the nearby land. The husband couldn't sleep because he heard these eerie sounds. Finally the husband, knife in hand, jumped into the river and tried to kill the woman. After his unsuccessful try, his body was never found.

After the story was spread around, people reported seeing her in different places. But the local people said that she appeared only on rainy, foggy nights.

55b 💀

As a young lady, I often met José in the grove of trees near the river. Much kissing and loving took place, but I was always careful to leave the area well before midnight. One night shortly before my engagement, time got away from me and I failed to leave before twelve. A cold chilling wind came up suddenly from the north with a furious intensity. A cat screamed, and a plaintive wailing sound came to my ears. It grew louder and louder until a blast of wind caused a white-robed figure to whisk past me. As the figure darted by, I saw that it had no face. I fell to my knees and sought God's help. Before long the wind stopped, and I could no longer hear the mournful cries. To this day, I have not returned to that cursed spot.

55c

Late one night, my uncle and one of his friends were coming home late from the cantina. They always took too much tequila, you know, and so it was pretty late. All at once, they saw this lady, about a block away, walking toward the canal. She really had a good figure.

Well, you know how guys are when they've had too much tequila—they get interested in the ladies. So they hurried to catch up, and they even called to her, but she didn't wait. She walked on down by the canal. Finally they were just a few yards away, and they called to her to wait. Slowly, she turned around—and she didn't have a face! She lifted up her hands toward them, and she had shiny claws, like tin. And she was coming toward them, like she was going to get them, you know.

Well, they turned and ran, with the woman right behind them, till they got to a bright streetlight, where she disappeared. My uncle never went to the cantina after that—He didn't want to meet La Llorona again.

56

Well, one time there was an old colored man lived over here—you talkin' about ghost stories—and he lived right close to my grandfather, and he worked for the Browns. The Browns owned a farm, and he was a hand on the farm, and my granddaddy lived right close to him, and he used to go down to talk with him some nights. They was great cronies.

So he goes down one night, and he had a big chat with my grandfather at headquarters. So as he was comin' on back home—They was always sayin' that there was ghosts, and he said, well, he was never scared of no ghost. So as he was comin' on back home, just between his home and my grandfather's—They had a big old tobacco house stood right on the side of the road. So as he's comin' on in the night by that, just as he got about the opp'site side of that old tobacco house, why there was a woman walked right out through the drawbars, right to the road, and he looked around and he looked at her, and he spoke to her and he says, "Is that you, Miss Dolly?" That's my mother. And he walked on, and she walked right along beside him, and he 'gin to walk a little faster and she did too.

So they went on about twenty yard, and he had a creek he had to go across before he got to his house. And as he walked a little faster, she did too, and so he struck a trot and she did too. So when he got to the creek he just lit out a'runnin' and he took right through the creek, and when he got through the creek she stopped. And he was out of wind.

He had just about twenty yards to go when he went to his house. And 'fore he got to the house he hollered for his wife, said, "Open the door, Ida!" And when he got to the door, 'fore she could open it, he fell agin' it and knocked the door open. And he fainted when he fell inside. And she run, "Lord, what's the matter?"

"Oh," he said, "there's sump'n got after me." Said, "There's some woman followed me up the road, but she never would speak and she disappeared and I don't know whar she went."

That was all I know. That happened down here—well, I'm fifty—I think that happened about sixty years ago.

57 ☠

This is a story about the old times. A long time ago, my daddy used to tell me about these old men that walk around on the road. 'Fore you know it, they had turned their head around backwards. One night my daddy and my brother, they were going down the road in Clarksdale. They were walking down the street on Hallowe'en night, and they see this man had turned his head around backwards. He was hollering like a cow. Daddy tried to catch him, and this man said, "You can't catch me. I'm a bad man. You can't catch me."

When he said, "You can't catch me," my daddy jumped on his back and tied him down and said, "Turn your head around back like it was."

And the monster turned his head. When he turned his head, my daddy knowed it was a old friend of his. He let the old man go, and he came back home.

58a ☠

One rainy and wintery night, a man was driving down this road and slowed up to come into this curve. As the headlights flashed around the curve, they showed that a young girl was standing in the road waving. The man stopped immediately and offered the girl a ride home, and she accepted by simply nodding her head.

The man was overwhelmed by the young girl's beauty and fell in love with her before she ever spoke a word. The young girl directed the man by pointing her finger and never saying a word. The man thought that she was just shy and didn't press a conversation. They finally reached her house, which was about five miles off the main highway, and the man got out to go around and open the door.

When he reached the other side of the car, he discovered that the young girl was no longer in the car. Thinking that she had already gone in the house, he went up and knocked on the door. An old, tired-looking lady came to the door and asked him in. When he asked to see her daughter, she looked surprised and began to explain that her daughter was killed on that very night just five years ago. She was on her way home from a party when it happened. She explained that this same thing had happened on the four previous years before now: she had been picked up, brought home, and disappeared for another year.

58b ☠

The story took place in Redfield, Arkansas, a little community about halfway between Pine Bluff and Little Rock, Arkansas. Supposedly, a man was driving along the road on a rainy, stormy night, and on the side of the road a young girl flagged him down. He stopped, and she told him that they had car trouble and would he give her a lift to her home. He agreed. So off they drove.

On reaching Redfield and pulling up in front of the house that she had pointed out, the man got out of the car, walked around the car to let the girl out. On reaching the other side and looking through the window, he discovered the girl had disappeared. The man was bewildered and confused. Not knowing what next to do, he walked up to the house and knocked.

A middle-aged couple came to the door, and he related the story to them of what had happened. They didn't seem to be too shocked. As a matter of fact, they told him that this had happened a number of times before on this particular date. And they went on to tell him that about four years before, their young daughter was out celebrating her birthday—that date—with her boyfriend. She was killed south of Redfield in a car wreck, along with her boyfriend. And they went on to tell him that this same thing had happened two or three times before, on this particular date. Evidently, every year on their daughter's birthday she would try to come home.

58c 💀

One night a man was driving along the highway between Little Rock and Woodson and noticed a girl standing on a bridge. He stopped and asked her if she wanted a ride. She explained that she was on her way home for the Christmas holidays and her home was just a few miles away in the small town of Woodson. Upon arriving at her home, she asked him to go to the door to see if anyone was there, because it looked very dark. Therefore, he went to the door and knocked, and when a woman came to the door, he explained to her that he had brought her daughter home for the Christmas holidays. The woman looked at him, astonished, and told him she was sorry but her daughter had been killed in a car accident one year ago from that very night. Puzzled, he went to the car and opened the door. There was nothing in the car but a coat. After carefully examining the coat, the woman stated that the coat was one of her daughter's.

58d 💀

There was a taxi driver, who, one day, after work was done, went on a spree. He drove all around the town, up one street and down another, and finally he came upon a dance. He stood for a long time in the doorway, seeing what he could see, and finally noticed a very pretty and charming girl. He went up to her and asked her to dance with him. She accepted, and they danced until very late. Then she decided to leave, and the taxi driver offered to take her home in his car. She accepted, and on the way home, she felt very cold. He took off the coat and gave it to her to put around her shoulders.

When they reached her home, she asked him to let her out at the garden gate. The girl got out, opened the gate, and went inside. The taxi driver went on home and went to sleep.

Next morning when he awakened, he recalled that he did not have his coat and decided to go to the girl's house to ask for it. He rapped on the door, and a woman answered. He said to her, "I'd like to speak to the young lady who lives here. We were dancing together last night."

The woman was a bit surprised and told him that her only daughter had been dead for many years. The driver protested that such was not possible, because they were dancing just last night and she had brought his coat home with her. The woman replied that she was sorry but that her daughter had died a long time ago. "Come with me," she said, "and I will show you her tombstone." So the mother and the taxi driver went to the cemetery. How surprised they were to find that upon the tombstone was hanging his coat!

The man fell ill, and a few days later he was dead.

58e ☠

In 1973, I was coming home late one Saturday night. As I approached the end of the bridge which leads out of Batesville, Arkansas, going towards Little Rock, a girl appeared. It looked like she came out of nowhere, and she was dressed in white. To avoid hitting her I had to slam on my brakes, real hard. I stopped the car and noticed the girl still standing there by the road. I noticed the girl's dress was long, white and torn. She had a cut above her eye. I asked her, "What happened?" She explained that she had been in a car accident and needed a ride home to get her father to pull her car out of the ditch it was in.

"OK, I'll take you home," I commented. "Are you OK?" She told me that she was fine and gave me the directions to her house. She did not talk any more. I took the directions she had given me to her house, but when I got there and turned around to say something to her, she was gone.

I knocked on the door. Her father came to the door. While I was trying to tell him what happened, her mother came to the door with a white dress and told me she had been killed two months before—in a car accident, the same place I had picked her up. I also learned that other people had seen her.

Now, on the night (anniversary) of her accident, don't be surprised if you see her yourself. She will appear just out of nowhere and ask for a lift. Oh, yes, she will be wearing white—a white dress—and it will be after twelve o'clock.

58f ☠

One time this man had been working late at night in his office and had to walk home because he had missed the bus. He was walking right by a graveyard and about to turn the corner when a lady stepped out and lit his cigarette that was hanging from his mouth. They began talking, and he asked her if he could walk her home. She said she would like that very much. The man walked her to her home, which was just a short distance away, and had a very enjoyable time.

The man enjoyed it so much that he decided to call on her the next night. He went to the house where he had taken her the night before and knocked on the door. A man came to the door and asked to help him. The man said he wanted to see his daughter, Anne. The owner of the house said, "You must be joking, my daughter has been dead for twelve years." The father took the man inside the house and showed him a picture of his daughter, Anne. It was the same girl he had walked home the night before.

The father said he would show the man her grave. They went to the grave, and there was her name on the tombstone. On top of the tombstone was a cigarette lighter that someone had left. The name on the lighter? Anne.

6 Malevolent Ghosts

Most ghosts are harmless to anyone with a clear conscience, but there are some that are vengeful and malevolent. Often the ghosts of dead lovers and husbands and wives return to haunt their faithless sweetheart or spouse. Second marriages of husbands or wives especially occasion spectral visitation. Sometimes it is a parent who comes back to make life unpleasant for his or her children; on other occasions the ghost returns to slay a wicked person or to take revenge on its murderer or on someone who injured or cheated it while it was alive. Frequently, the dead returns to punish a person who has stolen part of the corpse or who has in some way disturbed the grave; at other times it is to punish someone who is mistreating a relative. These are the major reasons for the return of vengeful Southern ghosts, some of whom are discussed in the following section.

It happened sometime in the late 1800s, in the summertime. A young man by the name of George Scott had been going with this girl, a lovely Southern girl, and she loved him dearly. They were planning to get married in the early fall. He decided for some reason that he...well, wasn't ready to get married and broke the engagement. She was just grief-stricken. Before long she became ill, caught typhoid fever, I think. She got worse and worse and finally died. He was upset about it, but not too much, because he went on with the other boys to see other girls.

Around Christmas, he and a bunch of young men were going to a party. They had to walk back home in those days. It was two or three miles on a narrow, winding road, so narrow only one buggy could pass and grown up on both sides. They had to go past the very graveyard where his girlfriend was. As they got right opposite the graveyard, they saw this funny-looking fog, a white form coming toward them. The other boys took off and flew, scared to death, and left him, but George Scott stood stock-still, petrified, because he knew who it was and it couldn't be anybody else. He didn't speak, and she didn't either. The white shape touched him. Its hand was icy cold. Then it vanished.

The others had gotten to the house, where they told what had happened and excited everybody. Some went back to see if they could find him, and they did. He was still in a daze. A few months later his health went bad, and he died young.

And that's not all. He was buried in the same cemetery not far from where the girl was. His parents put up a white tombstone about four feet high. After he'd been dead about forty years, the news got out that there was the likeness of that girl's face on his tombstone. It was some kind of discoloration, very visible, life-size. She'd been dead, of course, a long time, but people who'd seen her picture declared for sure it was she and nobody else. People came from miles around to see it.

60 ⚇

No sir, I don't reckon ghosts come out nowadays like they did two generations ago. Why, when I was a boy, folks in Rockford wouldn't go within hollerin' distance of the old graveyard after dark. In those days people really believed in ghosts, and from what I've seen I ain't exactly sayin' I don't.

Speakin' of ghosts reminds me of a story that's been told for years around Rockford. It's about an old fellow the kids called Still Face because he never smiled. He didn't have anything to do with anybody and lived with his old maid sister Hettie in a ramblin' house above the river. He had an old hound dog and spent a lot of time up the river huntin'. He was pretty fond of his sister, and they stayed at home most of the time. Folks didn't pay much attention to them.

Then one day Hettie took sick and in a week was dead. It almost killed old Still Face. He didn't have any other kin, so the folks got together and went to his house to make arrangements for the funeral and to sympathize with him. After the funeral the old man went home alone and didn't show his face for a week or so.

Then one night, about ten o'clock, old Charlie Wilson, who carried the mail from Yadkinville to Rockford in a two-horse wagon, was comin' up the road near the graveyard. He was late because a thunderstorm washed out the road pretty bad. It was lightnin' and thunderin' something awful, and old Charlie cussed and whipped the horses, tryin' to get in before the road got worse.

Well, just as the wagon got to the graveyard, there came a low, moanin' sound from among the tombstones. Charlie's hair stuck up. Suddenly the thunder crashed, and a flash of lightnin' lit up the cemetery. What he saw made him lose his false teeth and crack his whip on the horses' rumps. A human figure—ghost or livin'—was sittin' on top of a tombstone, right at the edge of the graveyard, with a rain-drenched dog beside him. Charlie didn't wait to see any more.

When Charlie got to town, everything was dark except a dim lamplight in old man Gink's store window. He went in breathlessly. When he told what he had seen, old man Gink swore it was only a tree swayin' or a stump or else some durn fool cuttin' through the cemetery on his way home. But didn't neither one of 'em figure that old Still Face might have gone out in the graveyard to his sister's grave and got caught in the storm.

Well, about three days later, along about midnight, a hound dog started howlin' over toward the old man's house. It kept howlin' all night, and folks thought it must be Still Face's dog. They could tell by its long, mournful howl that something was wrong. It didn't usually go on that way. The next mornin' some of the neighbors went over to the house, and sure enough, there was the old man lying in bed, deader'n a doornail.

Some of the pious citizens didn't want the old man buried with their kind in the graveyard because they figured he might contaminate their souls. So they decided to send his body to Yadkinville. They put him in a coffin and put it in the back of Charlie's mail wagon, which was leavin' for Yadkinville about four o'clock. There were no passengers for Yadkinville that day, so Charlie had to make the trip alone. He begged some of the boys down at the store to go with him, because he knew it would be dark before he reached Yadkinville. But none of them cared to ride with a corpse. As he was leavin', one of the boys hollered jokingly after the disappearing wagon: "The mail must go through, Charlie, so don't slack yer duty!"

Old Charlie whipped his horses into the river at Shallow Ford about sundown and was soon up on the other side, heading his wagon down the road toward Crutchfield and Yadkinville. He sat up in the front seat looking straight ahead, cluckin' his horses on and wishin' he could see somebody comin' down the lonesome road.

By the time Charlie had gone four miles from town, a cloud had come up and everything else black as pitch, except for a dim, flickerin' kerosene lantern swingin' on the side of the wagon. The woods on both sides were dark and still.

Then, suddenly, from the back of the wagon there came a low tappin' sound that got louder and louder, till it was an awful racket. It sounded like somebody strugglin' and kickin' to get out of a box. Charlie stiffened in his seat. That noise was comin' out of the coffin! Then came a ghastly shriek, and, with a crashin' of splinters, the coffin lid flew off.

Old Charlie jumped to the ground, and when he took his first breath he was half a mile down the road, runnin' like a streak of lightnin' toward Rockford. Me and some of the fellers was in the store when he staggered in, drippin' wet with sweat and muddy water. He fell into a chair, white as a sheet, and after catching his breath, told us what happened. Some of the boys said they didn't believe it, but I saw some doubtful looks in them fellers' eyes!

Next day, old John Borden, who lived on the island down the river, saw the horses, still hitched to the mail wagon, grazing on the other side of the river. The boys went over and found the coffin just like Charlie said. The lid was split, and the hinges had been broken off.

Nobody ever figured what happened to old Still Face. Some thought the old man wasn't really dead but had some sort of sleepin' sickness and, when he came to in his coffin, ran off into the swamp and died. Others thought the fellows had played a joke on Charlie. They figured some of 'em had carried the old man's body off and put one of the boys in the coffin.

Charlie quit the mail job and a few years later took sick and died. Nobody went near the graveyard on a dark night for a long time after that. Even now, when a storm comes up at night, and it's lightnin' and thunderin', a lonesome howl floats in from over the hills toward the graveyard, and the folks around town swear it's the ghost of the old man's hound huntin' for his master.

61 ☠

A long time ago there was an old Negro who had worked in a sawmill near Crossett all his life. He was very good at his job, and some of the newer Negroes thought he was a know-it-all, so they gave him a rough time. One day, the old man had taken all he could stand, so he hit the man who was fooling around with him, even though they were on the job. The young Negro struck back at the old one, knocking him into the buzz saw. The old man tried to break his fall with his hands, resulting in both of his arms being ripped off just below the elbow. The old Negro's life was saved, but he couldn't work in the mill anymore. The sawmill was his life, so he just wandered off and nobody ever heard of him again. Some time later, the young Negro who had started the fight was still working at the mill. He was found cut half in two by the saw. The Negro who was working with him at the time swore he saw two arms reach out of the shadows and push the screaming man into the buzz saw. Many other Negroes believed this also, but the judge at the murder trial didn't. The Negro was accused of murder and executed.

62 ☠

Back in 1925, after the El Dorado boom had settled down, there was a drilling company that pressured people into letting them drill for oil on their land. Now, many people were farmers, and they wanted to stay that way. Besides, most people knew how crooked this company was, so they didn't want any part of their business.

In one case, an old man had a farm out in the middle of the east field. The drilling company was reasonably sure there was oil on this land, but the old man didn't want his little farm turned into a mass of oil slick and salt flats. The men at the drilling company tried to reason with the old man, but he was stubborn. So they sent a bunch of roughnecks out to rough him up a little bit and try to convince him to sign with them so they could drill and collect their outrageous profits. But when they got out there, the old man grabbed a gun to protect himself, so the men had to kill him. He was found out in front of his house, lying in a large pool of blood.

The drilling company never did get to drill on the old man's property because the land was left to his son who lived in Chicago. The men never got convicted for the old man's murder, but later the drilling company got run out of town on other charges. So many years passed, and finally the son allowed the land to be drilled. The drilling crew had been working for days on the rig, trying to go down deep enough to hit the precious oil that no one could be sure was down there.

There was one older roughneck on the crew who, the men noticed, had been acting very strange ever since he started on this particular job. Every time he came out to the lease he started getting jumpy and afraid of every little thing. Then one night, the night shift was going about their normal tasks when a faint rumbling started deep in the ground. It got louder and louder. The well was coming in! The older roughneck stood there horrified while the other men tried to cap the well off before it gushered out over the top. But they weren't fast enough. The gusher rumbled and sprayed out the top of the derrick. The hard-working men were distracted by the older roughneck screaming, "It's blood! It's blood!" He fell screaming into the oily dirt and squirmed around as if he was being burned to death as the oil from the gusher rained over him.

Before the other men got the oil stopped it quit flowing of its own accord. This only meant one thing. There was not enough oil left in the hole to fool with. When they got back to the man lying in the dirt, he was dead. Later, everyone decided that the dead roughneck had had a hand in killing the old man some years back. Many people just figured that his conscience drove him crazy and he had a heart attack. But many people thought the old man's ghost came back to bewitch him and get revenge on him. Which do you think?

63 ☠

There is a terrible swamp out southwest of Magnolia called Bear Creek Bottom. It is full of quicksand, snakes and gators. Many years ago it was a lot wilder. One story about the swamp is that of a three-man search party.

Ever so often, someone would turn up missing after going hunting down in the swamp, either getting lost or getting killed by the animals and reptiles there. An old Negro who lived a little way down in the swamp knew his way around the swamp but wouldn't ever go down in it anymore because he thought the woods were alive. Everyone thought he was crazy, but they would get directions from him to go in.

Then one day, a man turned up missing who had three very close friends who went down into the swamp to search for him. They stayed in so long that people feared they were dead. Finally, one of the men staggered out of the swamp and fell alongside a road, where he was found. He had completely lost his mind; his whole body was cut up, and he had splinters stuck all in him, and his hair had turned white. He was mumbling that the woods were alive, over and over. Some people thought that he had seen his two friends die some terrible swamp death which had scared him out of his mind and caused him to run many miles through the underbrush. But many people remembered the old swamp nigger's warning, and they wondered if the very woods in the swamp were alive.

7 Witches, Banshees, Bloodstoppers, Ghostly Lights and Supernatural Creatures

To most Americans, witches are something out of the past, people who were charged with having, or claimed to have, certain supernatural abilities. Contrary to this notion, the tradition of witchcraft did not die in Colonial times but has persisted down to the present—and not just in out-of-the-way places but even in some of the largest cities in North America. Recently, in Miami, a man killed his wife reportedly because he thought she was a witch. Similar incidents have been reported from Indianapolis and Detroit, and in Georgia, a convicted murderess claimed to be a witch. One of Phil Donahue's recent shows was devoted to a discussion with four witches from a Wisconsin association of witches. Such cases are proof that there are people who strongly believe that witches and witchcraft are a real force in today's world. In folk tradition, the witch is generally a woman, often hideously ugly, usually using her supernatural powers for evil reasons. There are, however, also "white witches," who use their abilities for good.

While witches are common in Southern, and American, folklore, other supernatural figures are relatively rare. Certainly none of the European

*supernatural beings is less frequently found in this country than the ban-
shee, a type of bearer of bad tidings (usually a portent of death) who often
appears in legends from Wales and Ireland. They are not entirely unheard of
in this country, for Wirt Sikes reported in his book,* **British Goblins**
*(1880), an incident which happened in the 1870s in Evansville, Indiana: a
banshee appeared prior to the deaths of five members of the same family.
According to Sikes, "the circumstances attending the banshee's visits were
gravely described in a local journal as a matter of news." (p. 247) Still, it is
generally correct to say that banshees belong to old-world folk tradition
rather than that of the new.*

*While the banshee is not often reported in the South, ghostly lights,
supernatural creatures merely called "the thing," and bloodstoppers are.
Often the ghostly lights serve as omens, and "the thing" is usually sent to try
and make a bad person do better. Bloodstoppers—people possessing the
power to staunch the flow of blood from wounds or cuts, generally by means
of verbal charms that are effective against disease, evil and witchcraft—are a
different order of the supernatural. They use their powers on people for
reasons that most often have little to do with good or evil or how the person
receiving the charm has lived his life. Most of the charms date from pre-
Christian times but are revamped to fit Christian tradition. A majority of the
charms involve belief in the power of sacred or magic words, such as "Jesus,"
and usually only specially gifted persons can use the words effectively. A
person born with a caul, and a seventh son of a seventh son are both
supposed to be exceptionally skillful at bloodstopping. But even though the
belief in bloodstopping is common in America, relatively few examples have
been collected, due solely to lack of inquiry.*

*The few examples in the following section offer some representative stories
from the South about bloodstoppers, witches, banshees, ghostly lights and
other supernatural creatures.*

64 ☠

The muddy water of the Tar River in Edgecombe County near Tarboro moves sluggishly between the reedy, oak-shadowed banks as slowly and sullenly as it did centuries ago. The grist mill that once stood on the curve below the dam is gone, and no sign of the dam remains. But on misty August nights, when the yellow moon tilts on end and the rain crow calls for rain, the cry of the banshee that haunts the river splits the mist in a shrill, wild scream that echoes from bank to bank and dies away above the treetops in a throbbing, dismal moan.

During the Revolutionary War, David Warner, an Englishman, ran the Tar River mill. He was a staunch Whig and hated the English. He used his mill for the grinding of wheat and corn for the rebel army, furnishing them freely of his own food and allowing them to use the mill for grinding their grain. From dawn to sunset the mill clattered, the water turning the mill wheel often far into the night.

From the open door, the lantern light sent a golden path out into the darkness. Warner moved from hopper to bin and from bin to hopper, his shadow falling across the lantern glow, sometimes dwarfed and sometimes tall. He was a big man with a shock of black hair and black beard whitened with flour dust. His eyes were keen as an eagle's, and there was a fierce strength in his arms and wrists. He could lift a sack of grain with one hand and fling it over his shoulder, and with one turn of his wrist he could snap a tenpenny nail in two.

It was noonday in the heat of August. David Warner stood in the doorway of the mill listening to the lazy hum of jarflies and the raucous call of the katydids, when far down the road he heard the thudding sound of galloping horses. He knew before the runner came to warn him that the British were coming.

"Close your mill and hide. The British know you for a rebel, and they will kill you."

Warner looked at his big wrists and shook his head. "I'd rather stay and wring a British neck or two," he said grimly.

"But you can't stay and fight a whole army single-handed." The runner's teeth were chattering.

"Then," declared the miller, "I'll stay and be killed. What is my life?" He went back into the mill, and the runner followed.

The mill wheel was turning swiftly and Warner was sacking meal when six British soldiers crept to the door. Pretending not to see them, the miller said to the runner who was helping him, "Try to save every precious ounce of it, my lad, and we'll deliver it to General Greene. I hate to think of those British hogs eating a single mouthful of gruel made from America's corn."

When the soldiers heard this, they rushed in and seized the miller, cursing him for a rebel and beating him. Warner fought bravely, but five men held him fast. When they told him they were going to drown him in the river, he laughed in their faces and jeered, "Go ahead, go ahead, but if you throw me in the river, ye British buzzards, the banshee will haunt ye the rest of your life, for the banshee lives here. When the moon is dark and the river's like black ink and the mist is so thick ye can cut it with a knife, ye can see her, with her yellow hair falling about her shoulders, flitting from shore to shore, crying like a loon. And sure as the stars are in the sky, if ye drown me she'll get ye." Then he cursed them all 'round and dared them to carry out their threat.

For a moment the five men hesitated, whispering together. "Let's wait," said the tallest, "until the commander arrives. He will decide for us."

"Yes," agreed the second soldier, "let's wait."

But a big soldier with evil eyes and cruel mouth cursed and said, "Why wait? We are sent on ahead to make the way safe. We'll get rid of this rebel before he makes trouble."

The soldiers carried the miller down to the river bank. They bound his hands behind him. They tied a great stone around his neck and another to his feet. Then they threw him into the river. As his body sank from sight beneath the sullen water, a piercing cry ripped from the red clay ledges—the cry of a woman in the agony of death.

The soldiers stood frozen with fear. At first, there was nothing save a thick mist above the water. Then the mist took on the form of a woman with flowing hair and a veil for her face. The men turned white with horror.

"The banshee," whispered one. "The banshee," whispered another. But the soldier with evil eyes who had been so ready to drown the miller was too frightened to speak. He turned and fled to the mill.

At nightfall, the commander and his men arrived. The officers made their sleeping quarters in the mill house, and the soldiers pitched their tents beneath the trees. Soon campfires glowed against the night and made the shadows seem blacker. The new moon arose, tilted on end, thin and yellow. Far off a rain crow called for rain. From down the river came the banshee's cry—the cry of a woman in the agony of death.

The commander with his officers rushed from the mill house, and the soldiers ran from their tents—all except the soldier with evil eyes and his two mates who had helped him drown the miller. These three sat as if frozen, motionless, with their hands over their eyes, trying to stifle the agonizing wail.

The officers on the river bank saw a thick cloud of mist over the water; they saw it take the form of a woman with flowing hair and a veil for her face. When the soldiers climbed to the claybank ledge, no woman was there. The weird cry echoed far down the stream.

The three soldiers were so frightened that they confessed their crime. The angry commander, for their punishment, decreed that for the rest of their lives they should stay at the mill, grinding grain and listening to the haunting wail.

During the day they ground grain for the British, and at night the cry tormented them. Then one night the banshee came closer. She appeared in the doorway of the mill, a tall, mist-shrouded figure with flowing hair. She flung back her veil and faced the frightened men. The soldier with evil eyes cowered far into the corner, but the other two leaped to their feet, lured by the misty apparition before them. The banshee floated away just beyond their reach. Blindly they followed, heedless of where she led them. They came to the river. There they stumbled, fell into the water and were never seen again.

After that, the evil-eyed soldier who was left alone went raving mad. All through the night he wandered the woods, calling the miller's name. The cry of the banshee answered him. One day, his body was found floating face upward in the very place in the river where he had drowned the miller.

Years have passed, but to this day, in August, when the rain crow calls for rain and the moon is yellow and tilted on end, the mist will rise in a thick, white shroud. Slowly it will take the form of a woman with flowing hair and a veil for her face. Then sharp and shrill will come the banshee's cry—an agonizing wail that rises higher and higher, beating against the distance where it fades away in a dull, throbbing moan.

65 ☠

When the American colonies were being settled, Germans crossed the Atlantic, landed at Charleston. Then, as more and more arrived, they spread out over the state, living mostly along the rivers. Finally the area along the Saluda River was settled by German Lutherans. The Germans were Lutherans, you know. They were very law-abiding, good Christians; they read their Bibles regularly, they built churches and schools, practiced strict moral laws, attended church every Sabbath, prayer meetings every Wednesday night. They did every good deed possible; oh, they were a pious group, all right.

The old devil believed he could change them. So one night he really tried. Oh, he really tried to get in with these good people, so he dressed himself up; he looked like a—well, he was a good-looking man when he really dressed up and tried to date the girls; well, he did date the girls, but when they'd go out with him, they soon found out that he was the devil and they'd give him the kick. And then he tried the young men. He told them he knew where he could get something for them that would make them feel good and make them happy, and here he comes with a bottle of gin or liquor or whatever you call it and offered it to them, to see if he could make them drunk.

Oh, he did his best, but these were good pious people, and he couldn't make out, couldn't make them do anything he wanted them to do. Oh yes, he pretended to be a pious, Christian man too, and he went to church with them, especially on Wednesday nights, and oh, how he could pray! But he was a rascal, all right. They soon found out that he had the devil in him anyway. One time he asked a young lady to go horseback riding with him. That's the only way they had to go about in those days, you know. Anyway, even the horse knew that he was the devil; he threw him off.

So when he had tried every trick he could think of and failed, he really had to admit that he would have to give up. He was so angry that he was almost on fire. In the hurry to get out of the community, his burning feet set the woods on fire, and to this day one can see his track where he stepped on the large flat rock that lies on the hill between the Old Chapin Road and Wise Ferry Road, near the backwaters of Lake Murray and Old Tan Yard Creek.

66 ♟

Years ago the old log cabins, they didn't have locks on their doors like they have today. They had a hole honed through the door and through the door facing, and they run a chain through there and put a padlock on it, and they also had a hole in the door there where the cat could go in and out of at night.

And this one woman kept having this dream. She would dream of a night that she would hear the chains a'rattling on the door there, and every time it rattled, there would be a big black cat jump up on her head and get on her chest and it would just almost smother her to death. She said she just couldn't hardly breathe with the cat on there—was just like a dead weight. And this happened just night after night.

She finally told someone about it, some of the neighbors, and the neighbors that she told said, "You know this old lady that lives down the road here by herself, she is a witch, says she got mad at you about something, and this is her. She turned herself into a cat." And said, "The next time she does that, you get her by the foot and bite her, and that will stop her."

So the next night this woman went to bed and said just before she went to sleep, she heard the chains rattle and the door, and here come that cat and jumped right up on the bed and on her. It was so heavy she felt like it was going to mash her plumb through the bed, and said she couldn't hardly breathe. Said she grabbed the cat by its front paw and stuck its foot in her mouth and bit it real hard, and said the cat screamed out and squalled and jerked its foot back and took off out through the door. And she heard the chain rattle as it went out the door.

And the next day some of the folks walked by the house where the old lady lived down there and she had her hand all bandaged up, and she died just a short time after that. But she wore that bandage on her hand as long as she lived. After she died some of them took the bandage off, and there was teethmarks on her arm.

67 ♟

I've heard my father, Jesse Bolling, tell a tale about Jim Baker of Baker Flats. This Jim Baker was my great-grandfather. Now I don't know. I don't believe my father or mother would lie, an' I've heard them tell some awful tales about people being bewitched. They believed it. This one I'm goin' to tell was about Jim Baker.

He left my great-grandmother in North Carolina when my grandmother was a baby an' got him seven women and came back here an' lived in the Baker Rocks back yonder on top of Black Mountain. My folks thought he was a witch. After he'd finally left the flats an' settled on head of Cumberland, he married again an' settled down, but they still thought he was a witch. Father said that he was just a small boy, but Uncle Jerry and Uncle Jim were grown men.

One mornin' they heard a gun fire way back on Carmel Mountain, an' Granddaddy said, "That sounded to me like a witch's gun." Now they believed if a witch could fire a gun, as fer as it was heard the woods would be rung. That is, the ring within the sound of the gun would be bewitched, and nobody could kill a deer with his gun.

Well, Uncle Jerry went out a'huntin'. He saw some deer an' fired at 'em but didn't hit any. Hit was just that way on an' on. Uncle Jim went out, an' his gun wouldn't even fire. He had the lock an' powder pan worked on. He got new flints, but hit didn't do any good. So at last Granddaddy said he'd test it out. So he went out an' run tight up in a herd of deer. He was so close he could almost touch 'em, an' he was a dead shot. So he fired an' never hit a thing. He tried again. Same luck. Some pigeons lit in a tree, an' he fired at them an' killed one. He come back home an' went up on the point an' skinned the bark off a tree an' drawed the picture of Jim Baker an' stepped back fifty steps an' shot at it in the three highest names, Father, Son and the Holy Ghost, an' hit it.

He hadn't been back in the house when Jim Baker's wife come over to borrow some meal. They told her they were out. She went back, but hit wasn't long till she was back to borrow Grandma's winding blades. They were using them. The next morning', before they got out of bed, they heard her holler at the door, an' when they opened the door she was standin' there an' said, "Jerry"—that was Granddaddy's name—"if you don't come over an' do somethin' for Jim he won't be alive an hour."

He took a thumb lance an' went over there an' bled him a little, an' he got well right then. An' the spell was off their guns.

68 ☠

Jim Royal was an old slave that they claimed knew a lot about black magic. His people had learned it in Africa, brought it here with them. Now there's a legend about Jim Royal. I have heard old-timers, and I can remember back fifty years ago when these tales were current.

Jim Royal, they said, could take his violin and smash it over the back of a chair. It would fall to pieces. He would toss the pieces down, and it'd go back together again. 'Course that's a little hard to swallow and always has been. And they said his master would send him out to hoe corn. He'd go out to the fields to see how he's gettin' along. Jim would be up on the stump playin' the fiddle and the hoe just workin' the corn right along. 'Course that made him sort of a valuable slave, I guess. Hoe wouldn't get tired by itself.

So there were tales told about him that were remarkable. And now this incident I'm going to relate, it's not unknown today, and I guess the other things could be just as true—just as possible, rather. It seems he was always welcome as an entertainer at ev'ry gatherin'. There was some sort of mountain shindig, apple butter boiling' maybe or sump'n goin' on in a place over in Greene County, and Jim Royal was there. And they had heard that he could walk through fire, and he said he could. It seems that the information he give out was his own undoin'.

There was a big still on the fire and ev'rybody drinkin'. Mountain people always drink. So there's room enough under that still for a big log fire, great big still, you know. They had bonded stills in those days. So some of these people that claimed they knew Jim Royal could do it asked him to get back in this fire and play his fiddle. And they told the crowd, "He can play his violin back in that fire and won't singe a hair on his head nor one on the fiddle bow." And they all wanted to see it. Well, it was sorta cramped quarters under that still.

According to the legend, he made one condition which if he hadn't'a made he probably wouldn't've lost his life—that they throw no spirits on the fire; no whiskey to be throwed. And 'course whiskey was runnin' out the other end of the still by the bucketsful, runnin' off in wooden buckets and pour'd in barrels. And they claimed he got back under there and was playin' his violin when some of these big, rough mountaineers, probably drunk, picked this bucket of whiskey up from under what they called the worm of the still, walked around and threw it under there and burned him up.

That's the legend of the death of Jim Royal.

69 ☠

How Linkus Shiflett learned to play the fiddle from Jim Royal, that's what I'm comin' to now. Linkus never claimed to have any of the pow'r or the ability to do those kinds of things that Jim Royal had, but he did tell how he learned to play the violin. Now Linkus Shiflett was classed as a good man by all people that knew him. He had that reputation: a kind man and certainly not a liar as far as I could ever learn. And they asked him how he acquired such a talent. They say he was wonderful, just a mountain boy, you know, grew up a mountain boy. First violin he ever had he had to make out of a gourd.

So he told me, after Jim Royal was gone, that he had asked Jim Royal if he could teach him to play the violin like he did. He said, "If you wanta go through the ordeal that it would require," said, "yes, you can be as good a violinist as I am." And he asked him how. He designated an old outhouse somewhere. They built outhouses in those days for smokehouses or to put root crops and vegetables in and things like that.

Jim Royal told him to bore nine holes through an ironwood tree, that was the first process, to bore nine holes through this ironwood tree. And ev'ry mornin' for nine mornin's he was to go and run his fiddle bow through all those nine holes nine times each. And there was various other things that he was required to do that have slipped my memory now, but the one that stands out the most is the last one he was told.

He said, "Now you have one more test." And he designated this old outhouse that Linkus must go to on a certain day and he must never speak. When he got out he wasn't to speak until he got back home. And he said he must stand his ground no matter what he saw or what happened, he mustn't speak or he mustn't move. So, accordin' to the legend, Linkus said that ev'ry horrible thing imagined would come in that outhouse and said he stood shakin'. But he said part of the time he was paralyzed and couldn't move. But said he stood it all until at last a big black snake crawled through the logs and come in and began to wrap himself around his neck and he started to put his head in his mouth—he was standin' there with his mouth open—and said he broke down and shook the snake off and broke and run.

And so when he saw Jim Royal again, he told him about it. Said, "I stood my ground for ev'rything else, but I couldn't stand the snake puttin' his head in my mouth."

"Well," he said, "you got to go through with it all or you'll never learn to play."

And he wanted to play the violin so bad he set another day to go. He said that time he stood his ground and said it was worse, ev'ry hideous thing that he could imagine come into that building to torment him. And last thing, the snake come in again and he crawled up, and when he crawled up that time the snake put his head clear back to his throat three times and dropped to the ground, crawled away, was nothin' there. Linkus said he went on back home.

From then on, he said, he could play the violin as good as Jim Royal. And he was a famous violinist for these mountains. So that was his version of how he acquired his ability to play the violin so well. My grandfathers have heard him play. Some of the old-timers that I knew have heard him play.

70 🩸

Well, I never knew George Herring myself. He was a supposed wizard. I knew his sons, Jake Herring and Noah Herring. I knew their children and their grandchildren. I went to school with their children—with George Herring's grandchildren. But George Herring didn't live too far from where we lived in Greene County. We lived at the base of the mountain in Shiflett Hollow on the Simmons Gap Road after you cross the mountain.

The legend I heard of George Herring begins with another man—an old Negro that used to live close to George Herring after the Civil War, Old Solomon. Whatever other name he had I never learned. So it was claimed that Old Solomon was—well, the folks called him a witch. He was supposed to be a warlock or a wizard. He's a black man, and he and George Herring had some difficulty somewhere along the line.

Herring's cattle began to come up, and he noticed a chalk mark or sump'n across a path in his field that these cattle come in on from pasture, and he said as fast as his cattle come up, accordin' to the tale, they dropped dead right in the barnyard. Had four or five all died right there. And he said he searched the field and he found different symbols and things across these cowpaths, and he said he knew that Old Solomon had killed 'em.

So George Herring, accordin' to the legend, knew he couldn't do anything with Old Man Solomon, not havin' enough power to counteract it, and he decided to leave. He was gone for a long, long time, and none of his family ever knew, but he went to learn more about black magic. Where he went he knew of a man that was supposed to possess magic powers, that dealt in black magic. But anyway, he came back a lot smarter man in magic than he left home.

The children was there when he came back. That night he made all the family go to bed. He dared anyone to even speak. In those days the family usually slept in one big room or some up in the attic, you know. The houses built different—old-timey houses. And they built up a log fire in the fireplace. Fireplaces and chimneys were huge in those days. And he sat down in a chair in front of the fire and he drew symbols all around on the floor. Said he sat there till midnight watchin' the clock and said at midnight a black cat come down the chimney through that fire and landed out in the floor toward these symbols. He kicked it back into the fire and stomped it into the fire, but it got away and went back up the chimney.

And next mornin' some of Solomon's relatives or his family came to borrow, and they kept comin' to borrow, and Herring dared his family to loan 'em anything. The last thing they come after was a needleful of thread and they were refused. And the next mornin', they said, accordin' to legend, Old Solomon was burnt to death. So that's taken with a grain of salt, but most people in those days believed it and they said Old Man Solomon was suddenly burned up. They had a doctor and he died from it next mornin'. People that knew George Herring, I've heard 'em tell it.

---

71 ☠

I used to hear 'em say there was a fellow lived in here, they called him, let's see, Jim Royal. He was colored. Said he was a little-bitty nigger and said he looked just like a man like everybody else. Said he used to have a little white horse, just as white as snow and the purtiest thing. He used to ride on that horse, and he'd sail—said he'd just actually sail in the air on that horse. Anybody'd get after him or the law would get after him for anything he'd do, he'd take a little switch and touch that little white horse on the flanks and he'd holler, "Up we jump, and here we go." And said that little horse would get up and just sail through the air. 'Course that was 'fore my time, but I heard the ancestors say he could fly on his horse and he was a great fiddle player and he could do more kinda magic tricks.

Jim Royal's daddy was gonna whip him one time. Said his daddy went to beat on him, and he looked and he was beating a stump and Jim Royal was up on the hill laughin' at him. He must have been the devil.

Jim Royal played a fiddle quite a bit, and they said he could set up in a brush pile; they'd set the brush pile afire, and he'd be playing his fiddle and he could vanish. He'd set on a stump and play with the fire burning all around him; he wouldn't burn playing his fiddle while the fire was burnin' all 'round him, and first thing you know Jim Royal'd be vanished.

'Course you know that was fairy tales they was tellin', but the old people say it was so. All that was handed down, and they believed all that stuff about Jim Royal.

72 ☠

It's just like Old Lady. I was a girl then. And so Ernest Nole and his wife come to visit Ernest's people. And the old lady was named Old Lady Lizzie. And there was a man by the name of Frank Roberts, and she was riding him every night. She would ride him. And so he asked one of the boys to come and spend the night with him.

Said, "I just don't feel like spending the night."

Said, "Well, please come stay. It's a witch riding me every night." And said, "I want you to get a big stick."

See, people didn't have brooms with handles in 'em like now. They swupt with fennel leaves or weeds and broom straws; they didn't have brooms with handles in 'em like they got now. They go out in the fields and things and get this old dog fennel; they called 'em old yellowtops. Said he gone get them and that's what they used for brooms. So he say, "I want you to get a good seasoned stick."

So he did. So they laid down. You know, they tell me you be makin' a fuss tryin' to get up but you can't. See, it be like— something like to smother you to death. And said, "Now, but you hear me make that fuss," he said, "then you hit her." And when he started making that funny fuss, he struck her. And she was an old lady, and she went home. And she sicklied and died; she never did get over that hit. It kilt her. That's right; it kilt her.

73 ☠

It was a long time ago, when people first came from eastern Virginia and western North Carolina and settled here in the Cumberlands. A settler, whose name has been forgotten, had a large flock of sheep. Suddenly his sheep began to die, one a day, seemingly from no particular cause. He watched his flock and would see a ram or ewe suddenly fall dead while it was feeding along in the best of health.

He believed his sheep were bewitched so he hied himself to an old woman who was reputed to be a witch doctor. She told him to go home and skin out the ham or shoulder of a sheep that had just died and put it in an oven and bake it and by no means allow anyone to come in the house and borrow, steal or in any way get anything out of the house, above all a drink of water. So he skinned a sheep that had died that same day and put a shoulder on in the oven to bake. The witch doctor had said to let it warm up slowly and start baking gradually for best results. He followed the directions, and it was two hours before the shoulder was warmed up to the baking stage.

About that time he looked down the road and saw a neighbor woman coming, walking as if she was in a hurry. She came on, entered and asked to borrow some meal. They had no meal. She then asked for a drink of water; and there was no water up. She took her departure, but in a short time she was again seen approaching, walking faster than before. This time she seemed unstrung and could not stand still and wanted to borrow some salt—no salt in the house; and again she asked for water, which was politely but firmly refused her. All the time she was eyeing the oven on the hearth, and this time before she left she asked what they were baking and tried to accidentally overturn the oven.

She had not been gone long until she was seen coming again. This time she was running. The shoulder was getting a nice brown now. She rushed into the house and screamed, "For God's sake, get that off there! You are killing me. Look here!" And she ripped off her clothes and exposed her own shoulder baked to the same crisp brown as the mutton shoulder. The woman recovered, but if she ever practiced her witchery again it was not found out.

74a ☠

There was this girl who lived next door or behind my grandmother's house in Juarez. She wasn't too old and was very pretty. She didn't like to do what she was told. If her mother said to do something, she wouldn't, even if it was something that she really wanted to do. She wasn't old enough to go on dates, but she was pretty enough.

One night she told her mother she was going to El Gato—that's a bar where they go to dance and it's not very clean and you've probably never heard of it—and dance with her boyfriend. Her mother was so mad that she shut the girl in her room and went to a bar herself. The girl sneaked out a window and went to El Gato with her boyfriend, and while they were dancing, she saw this good-looking man dressed in green come in. He smiled at her, and she went right over to him and danced with him for a long time. He was real good-looking, but he had a limp and he could still dance.

When it was late, she decided to go home because her feet were tired, and he was going to take her. When they got outside, people heard a loud scream and ran out. The girl was all scratched and bloody on the sidewalk, and a rooster was flying down the street. As she died, she said, *"Eres pata de gallo."* This means that it was the devil, because he is always a cripple in the left foot. The people got out their rosaries and started saying them and ran home.

The next day the sad mother came and took her body to bury. She told the girl, "I told you not to go out, or the devil would get you." The priest would not bury her in the cemetery, and so they just dumped her in the desert for the coyotes.

My grandmother told me this story as the truth, but I don't really think that they just dumped the dead body on the desert. That's against some law.

74b ☠

There was a girl living in the house next door to my aunt. She was very pretty but too young to go on dates. One night she went to the Acapulco Bar on Pershing Drive to dance and have a good time. Her mother had told her not to go because it was Friday and she had to go to church. She went anyway. There she met a dark, handsome man who danced every dance with her.

After the bar closed, he was going to walk her home. All of a sudden, he was sort of like a goat and danced all over her with his hoof. *Pata de chivo*, it is called. She saved herself by taking out her rosary and showing it to him. He ran away, but she was almost dead and had to have a lot of sewing done on her where he tramped. She still has a hoof-shaped scar on her face, but now she goes to church every Friday and is very obedient.

This story tells what will happen if you don't mind the teacher and your mother.

74c ☠

Once there was a girl who lived near my grandmother. I didn't know her, but my aunt did. She was very pretty, and all the men liked her and tried to date her. She didn't help at home. Her mother worked very hard in El Paso so that the girl could have nice things and go to school. The girl wanted to go to a cantina and dance one night. The mother was very tired and asked the girl to stay home and take care of her little brother. The girl wouldn't. She went to the cantina and danced with all the men.

Finally a stranger came in. He was very good-looking and walked with a slight limp. He passed all the other girls by and danced only with this girl. He seemed very rich, and the girl was very interested in him. While they were dancing, someone tore his trouser leg, and everyone could see the *pata de gallo*. Someone screamed, and the lights went out.

When the lights came on, the girl was half in and half out of the door, and she had been scratched to death. As the people picked her up to carry her away, they heard a loud laugh and a cock crow. It had been the devil.

74d ☠

There was a girl at Jeff who wanted to go to a dance real badly. Her mother said she couldn't go because she was sick and wanted her to stay home with her. So she locked herself in her room, got dressed, turned out the lights as if she had gone to bed, and slipped out of the window.

She was walking down the street when a good-looking guy passed in a convertible. He passed her a couple of times and then stopped and asked her if she would like a ride. She said no. Then he asked her where she was going, and she told him to the dance. He said wasn't that funny, that was exactly where he was going, too. So he gave her a ride to the dance.

They got to the dance and were dancing one of those fast rock-and-roll dances, and he was turning her around and around. Somehow he had danced her outside into the alley. All of a sudden, the people heard loud, terrible screams from outside! They went out and found the girl had been all scratched and torn, and her face was all torn and bloody. Next to where she was, there was a bush that was all on fire and glowing. They knew then it was the devil! The girl died.

74e ☠

There was a girl who was married but was living with her mother because her husband was overseas. She wanted to go to a dance one night, but her mother forbade her to do. She fought with her mother and hit her. As the mother was dying, she moaned and moaned.

The girl went to the dance anyway. She danced with a handsome man who was dressed in a tuxedo. Suddenly the lights went out, and when the girl looked down, she saw that he had feet like a rooster, and she knew he was the devil. Before she could get away from him, he scratched her face real bad and made moaning noises like her mother had.

I know this is true because I saw her the next day, and her face was all covered with little tiny scratches.

75 ☠

Well, my dad had a GE place that burned about six years ago. My dad had a picture of his dead brother on his desk, and it did not burn. The picture was taken a few days before my uncle died in a car wreck. The picture was made for Janet. Dad asked for a copy, but he got the real one and Janet got the copy.

After that Mom got a real nice frame for it. When it was dark, the frame sort of shined. People have even tried to burn the picture with a match or lighter. The thing just won't burn. Mom started getting scared; she told Dad that the picture watched her all the time. So to please Mom, Dad put it away in a box of pictures. Now it can't be found. That is strange.

76 ☠

I was coming down the highway, and a little boy got hit by a truck. He would have bled to death. I was the third car. The truck hit him just as he got across from the school, right across the road. He saw the truck coming, and he thought he could make it.

And I walked up to the kid. He was bleeding out his ears, out his mouth—It looked like everywhere he was bleeding. And I walked up there, and I gave these words. And then this white fellow that hit him pushed me, and he says, "We're going to put him in this truck."

I said, "No, you're not." I said, "You're not going to put him in the truck. I'll put him in my car. He's not too bloody. You gonna put him back there where those animals been?" He'd been haulin' animals.

I put a sack or something down there, you know. I decided to put him in my car. By that time another car came up, and they took him here to a doctor before he, uh, bled to death...I stopped the bleeding before they picked him up. You see, he had lost so much blood, they couldn't give him blood fast enough. They rushed him to Albany. And he died in the Albany Hospital.

But had he been in my car he wouldn't have never bled that much.

77 �

This girl up on the hill here, she came out here one afternoon and she said, "You know what?" She said, "Precious, I've been worried all day. You know Minnie Mae Wooders? Did you know I saw her last night in a pool of blood?" Said, "I don't know how she got hurt or what happened to her. I've been tryin' to call her, and I haven't gotten her yet."

I said, "Well, just keep tryin', 'cause she might be sick."

You know where she was? Went to a funeral down there at Valdosta, and somebody ran into their car and she was drivin' the car. And they took 'em all to the hospital there.

Now she foresaw that.

78 ☠

I had a sister one time that knocked a window stick out—was propped up like that window there—knocked out, and some way or other she bit a big artery in her tongue. Bit it plumb in two. 'Bout nine o'clock one morning. And she bled until nearly sundown, and just about bled to death.

And there was a fellow on up above us named Charlie Williams. And my uncle, I remember, he rode a horse up there, and just about the time he got there, had time to ride the horse up there, the blood stopped. The doctors had tried all day to stop it, and they hadn't stopped it. And that blood clotted on her tongue. And the next morning it come loose, and she swallowed it and it like to choked her to death. And that thing never did bleed no more. Now I know them things.

79 ☠

I was batchin' then, up there in Virginia. Been out on my horse, and my little old dog had followed me. When I got to the lane—guess I was about two hundred yards from the end of it—I spied two men. They was walkin' together purty fast, keepin' step. I watched 'em. They had four times as far to go as I did. I kept on watchin' them an' never took my eye off of 'em till they got to the lane. Then the little old dog jumped a rabbit, and I turned to look. That quick they disappeared or turned into somethin', one. They was a black thing about the size of a sheep thrashed around an' took up through the field, tearin' up brush heaps where there wasn't no brush heaps an' makin' a lot of noise. It didn't look like nothin' I'd ever seen. Don't know what it was, but they had turned into it.

I went on an' got to the Anneson bottom. Crossed it, an' it was gettin' dusk. Somethin' began to make a noise under my mare's nose. Couldn't see a thing, but I watched for the black thing to show up again. I went on through, an' a light flashed. It scared the mare, an' she started runnin', run till I got hold of the bridle and quieted her down. Never could tell what it was.

80 ☠

When I was fourteen, a young fellow came up to the house courtin' me. I stayed in the kitchen because I didn't like him, but after a while he came around to the back door and told me to see the light out there in the field.

I stepped outside. There was a big ball of fire comin' up the lane at our landlord's house next door. Our landlord was Barry Nelson. That light danced up to the gate and went out until it got right over the house. It came back on then and came down and touched in the field by the house. Then it went back the same way it had come. Yep, back over the house and up the lane.

The next day a woman that lived in that house was chopping cotton in that same field. When she got to the spot where that light touched down, she fell over dead. That's right—at the exact spot where that light touched down, she fell over dead. I saw it.

8 Grave Humor

Although many ghost stories and tales of the supernatural are related to provoke fear or prove the existence of ghosts, a large number are also told for humorous effect. Ray B. Browne, in **"A Night With the Hants"** and **Other Alabama Folk Experiences** (1977), says that approximately half the stories told in Alabama on death and the hereafter are humorous. He attributes this high percentage to an attraction/repulsion with death and the dead. There is a morbid, almost pathological, interest in corpses, ghosts and hants, but at the same time there is a realization that there is something unhealthy about such interest. Thus, the comical treatment arises as a means of balance. Browne's statistics don't seem to hold up in other Southern states (although no one has really bothered to make a count), but his reasons for the existence of humorous narratives about ghosts and the like may have great validity. Whatever the case, the following section includes some examples of Southern grave humor.

Once there was an old man who grew queer in his old days, and when he died he asked that a peck of hickory nuts be buried under his head so he could crack them and eat his favorite delicacy when he became hungry.

Two thieves lived in the community, and one night they decided to steal a sheep. One of them was to wait in the graveyard while the other went up on the hillside and picked out a choice sheep and brought it down.

While the rogue waited in the graveyard, he happened to think of the hickory nuts underneath the dead man's head, and being hungry and having some little time to wait, he dug them up and began to crack them leisurely. Two farm boys happened to pass near the graveyard just then and they heard the cracking. They went home swiftly.

"Grandpap," they said, "old Jim Higgins is risin' out'n his grave and cracking the hickory nuts under his head."

"Nonsense," said the old man, "I don't believe it."

The boys swore that it was so.

"Don't believe it," said the old man, "and if I didn't have this rheumatism that's had me down for the last ten years I'd go and see for myself."

The boys considered for a moment and finally answered. "Grandpap, we'll carry you on our shoulders if you want to see it," they said.

"I'll go on your shoulders to show you there's nothing there," said he. And he got ready to be carried on their backs to the graveyard.

When they came near enough to hear the cracking, they walked stealthily·and crept very close to the fence and might have seen the grave of Jim Higgins if the bushes hadn't been hiding it. There was silence for a time, and then there was rustling down the hillside, and the thief with the sheep appeared from behind the clump of bushes. The white sheep, from that distance, loomed up as a ghost and seemed to rise and swell to magnanimous proportions before the startled eyes of the two boys and their grandfather. The rogue who was cracking hickory nuts was unaware that the visitors were near. He ceased cracking when he saw the sheep. "Is he fat or lean?" he asked.

The spoken word was all the boys needed. They then threw the old man to the ground and addressed the ghost.

"Fat or lean, take him!" they said and ran for home.

As they reached the porch, one of them said, "Boy! I bet that ghost has done got Grandpap."

"He ain't either," said the old man from inside the house. "I beat you in."

82 ☠

Well, this is a small story about a fellow called Graveyard John. Ole Miss died, and John worked around the house. At that time, it wadn't no funeral home, and they had Ole Miss there in the house. Ole Miss had on some diamond rings and things, and John was spotting that stuff. He supposed to been sweeping up, but the people that was in the waiting room say, "John, keep a'sweeping now."

"Yes ma'am, Ole Miss, I'm sweeping."

He'd sweep and peep through the crack.

Say, "John, why don't you go on and sweep. I want you to git everything cleant up 'fore all the visitors git here."

"Yes ma'am, Ole Miss, I'm sweeping." So John peeped through the crack. He shake his head and say, "I'm gonner git that tonight"—talking 'bout them watches and rings.

Finally, John got everything cleaned up and that night he went to the cemetery to dig Ole Miss up. Ole Miss wadn't dead. She had went off in a trance. John, he got the top off the box, and he got his head down in there, and he thought he heard something, and he jumped up out the grave. He say, "Aw, naw. That wadn't nothing. I'm going back there. I'm gonner git them rings. I ain't gonner let nothing scare me off of them rings."

John went back there, and he got one of the rings, but one ring was on there so tight he couldn't git it. When he tried to git that one off, Ole Miss clamped him, and out the grave he come with her on his back. John wadn't hollering nothing but "Dey! Dey! Dey!"

She fell off at they house, and when she went in that upset the family. Say, "Oh, what you doing here?"

Say, "John saved my life. Wherever he is, don't y'all bother him, because he saved my life."

Say, "Well, we'll try to find him. I hope he don't run clean off."

"Well, I do too."

So the next day they set out to look for him. They say, "Y'all talk to him easy. You might git up to him."

They got out there and found him in a sage field. Say, "Here we lay right here." They went there and they talked to him and say, "John."

"Dey. Dey. Dey. Dey. Dey. Dey. Dey."

"John, we ain't gonner bother you."

He jumped up and said, "Dey! Dey! Dey! Dey got me!"

---

83 💀

I heard my father tell a story one time. He was born and raised in Logan, West Virginia, and he never did go back to his hometown after he married my mother. He said that they had a big house one time, and these people thought it was haunted. And they hired him and another guy to watch it. Fifteen or twenty dollars back in those days was worth a hundred now. And they watched this house that night, and he said they was laying there that night and there was a noise like a man walking through the house, and my dad said he was so scared he didn't know what to do. Sounded just like this man walkin' over the floor. And they watched and watched and they couldn't find out where it was coming from or where it was going, and finally they found what it was making all the noise. Somebody had caught a muskrat in the house and this steel trap had growed in its leg and it learned to walk with that steep trap. And every time it walked, it would make this noise. My dad showed it to this man and they stayed a couple of nights afterwards and found that they had really caught whatever it was that they had caught.

---

84 💀

Now an old man was going through the country, and he come to a house and he asked if he could stay overnight. The man told him he didn't have room in his house, but that there was a house on down the road he could stay in but that the house was haunted.

The old man said he wasn't afraid of hants, and so he went on down the road until he came to this house. It was about dark when he looked in. But there was a lamp sitting by a table, and so he went inside, lit the lamp and sat down in the chair.

Well sir, we sat there and nothing happened until nearly midnight, and then a big black cat poked his head in at the door and said, "Me-ow!" And the man, he didn't say anything. The big black cat walked all around in the room and then hopped up on the table, wrapped his tail around the lamp and just lay there a'lookin' at this man with them big green eyes he had.

About then the man heard a *thump, thump, thump,* upstairs in the loft, and then a *thump, thump, thump,* on the stairsteps, and a man's head rolled down the stairsteps right into the room. Yes sir, it did, a man's head, and it stopped rolling, and the eyes in that head looked right at the man in the chair.

But this man didn't say anything, he didn't, and then he heard *thump, thump, thump,* again on the stairsteps, and a man with no head came down the steps. A man with no head, yes, and this man with no head walked over to the man in the chair and he said:

"Two of us here, I see."

"Yes," said the old man, "but there ain't goin' to be very long."

With that, he jumped as far as he could out the door, and he started running, and he ran and ran until he was plumb give out, and he sat down on a log to rest, and in a little while the man with no head sat down beside him and said:

"Had a pretty good race, didn't we?"

"Yes," said the man, "an' we're goin' to have another one."

So he jumped up from the log and he ran out of the woods into a corn field, and a rabbit was running there, and the man said to the rabbit, "Get out of my way, rabbit, and let somebody run that can run."

85 🁢

This man was walking through a graveyard one night, and he accidentally fell in an open grave. The grave was so deep that he was unable to get out by himself in spite of his many attempts. The caretaker was off duty that night, and no one was there to hear his cries for help. It was real cold that night, and by morning he was nearly frozen. He heard someone coming through the graveyard and cried out to him:

"Help! It's cold down here!"

The man passing through came up to the grave and, looking down, said, "I guess so, someone took all the dirt off you."

Notes

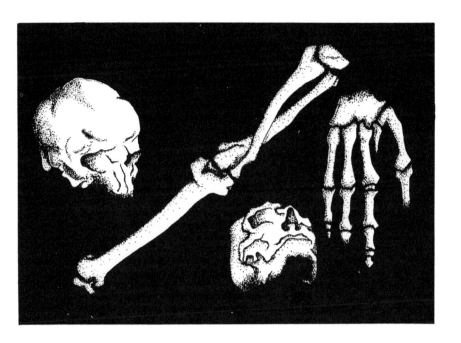

In the following notes as much detail is given on the informants as is available to me. This includes name, age, place of collection and residence, attitude towards the narratives, manner which the text is generally used, and other biographical material. Where any of these features are absent it is because they were not supplied by the collectors. Some fieldworkers provide copious accompanying information with their texts while others give nothing more than the informant's name. Early collectors, such as those working for the WPA in the 1930s, were particularly guilty of paying little attention to such matters. Happily, most of the collectors whose work is utilized here were cognizant of the necessity for such accompanying details. Earlier folklorists were mainly concerned with texts rather than context while more recent scholars realize that both are important.

At the end of the comments about the texts are motif numbers. These refer to the systems employed in Ernest W. Baughman, **Type and Motif-Index of the Folktales of England and North America** (The Hague: Mouton & Co., 1966) and Stith Thompson, **Motif-Index of Folk Literature,** 6 volumes, revised edition (Bloomington, Indiana: Indiana University Press, 1955), the standard indices of narrative elements found in American folk tradition. Baughman's numbers are cited first because he is more directly concerned with American folk narratives, but in some cases, he *does not list parallel material. In these instances Thompson's numbers are given. References to type numbers refer to Stith Thompson's* **The Types of the Folktale** *(Helsinki: Suomalainen Tiedeakatemia Academia Scientiarum Fennica, 1961).*

1. Collected in 1974 by Wanda Lee Johnson from a sixty-one year old with businesswoman identified only as Mrs. D. B. of Paragould, Arkansas. The informant is the daughter of the family who lived in the house, and her older sister, the child of the story, also believes that the story is factual. Johnson titled this "The Legend of the Door That Refused to Stay Closed" but that seems to be her own contribution, for there is no evidence that the informant had any specific name for it or that she even referred to it as a legend. The narrative serves as incontrovertible proof of the existence of ghosts and witchcraft for both the informant and her sister.

For those unfamiliar with the term "ticktacking," it is a word referring to a type of practical joke played by many young pranksters. By means of a controlling cord and weight, a device is rigged up whereby a person can tap on windows and house walls from a distance. The name probably comes from the sound made by the device when it is in operation.

Although the informant referred to this as a ghost story, it is really a story of witchcraft, the ghost only being mentioned at the very end of the narrative and then only as a suspicion, not something that had been sighted. The tale is reminiscent of the Faust story (motif M22 "man sells soul to devil") in that the painter claimed to have acquired his powers directly from the devil and, in order to do so, presumably had to sell his soul. Also pertinent are motifs D1273 "Magic formula 'charm'"; D1710 "Possession of magic powers"; E281 "Ghosts haunt house"; G224.4 "Person sells soul to devil in exchange for witch powers"; G265.8 "Witch bewitches objects"; G265.8.5(b) "Witch bewitches house"; G265.8.3.2 "Witch bewitches wagon"; G249.8 "Witches open doors and windows"; G269.5 "Witch causes haunted houses"; and Thompson's D1641.13 "Coffin moves itself" and F1083.0.1 "Object floats in air."

It is interesting that the son of the house's builder believes none of this story.

2. Collected March 1, 1978 in Henderson, Kentucky, by Nana Farris from Mrs. Frank Reed, Sr. The informant was discussing a series of personal experiences that occurred while she and her family lived in an old two-story log house during the years 1914-1916. Mrs. Reed frequently laughed during the course of telling her experiences, the laughter evidently a nervous reaction rather than an indication that the tale was humorous and not to be taken seriously. Reed evidently tells of her experiences as a testimony in favor of belief in the supernatural. Apparently she is a skillful narrator because she made use of vocal dynamics to point out significant points in her narrative and she imitated the voices of characters, such as her boyfriend, who figure in the tale. She also made use of hand gestures to indicate such activities as spinning and drawing bed covers back.

Motifs include E279.3 "Ghost pulls bedclothing from sleeper"; E402 "Mysterious ghostlike noises heard"; E402.1.3(b) "Ghost plays organ"; E423.1.1 "Revenant as dog"; and E561 "Dead person spins"; E545 "The dead speak." An incident similar to the talking sounds heard by Mrs. Reed appears in Ray B. Browne, *"A Night With the Hants" and Other Alabama Folk Experiences"* (Bowling Green, Ohio: Bowling Green University Popular Press, 1977), p. 27. Thompson's E545.1 "Conversation between the dead" is also relevant.

3. Collected September 3, 1965, by George Foss from Lloyd Powell, Browns Cove, Virginia. Powell was born in Browns Cove in 1905 in a house that had been in his family since the 1860s and continued to live in the same community until his death in 1977. In his later years he lived with his sister Hilma Powell Yates in a building that originally served as the overseer's home for a large plantation/farm once owned by their family. The main house of the property was called "Headquarters" because for a brief period during the Civil War it had been used by Stonewall Jackson as headquarters for his troops who were on their way to help Robert E. Lee defend Richmond. Apparently, Powell related this tale primarily as an example of the sort of narratives about the supernatural once commonly told in his community. In other words, it was both entertainment and an important bit of local history for him.

The only relevant motif is E402 "Mysterious ghostlike noises heard."

4. Collected March 27, 1977, by Debbie McWilliams from Kathy Thornton in Tuscaloosa, Alabama. Thornton, from Huntsville, apparently is a relative of the family that currently owns Cedarhurst, the house in which the supernatural incidents concerning Sally Carter took place. As the last line indicates, Thornton thinks many of the stories about Sally are absurd. Still, she firmly believes her cousin's experience and that of other family members, even though she probably recounts them mainly for entertainment.

Motifs include E235.6 "Return from dead to punish disturber of grave"; E281 "Ghosts haunt house"; E281.0.3* "Ghosts haunt house, damaging property or annoying inhabitants"; E402.1.7 "Ghost slams door"; E419 "Other restless dead"; and E422.4(a) "Female revenant in white clothing." The idea of a ghost returning to see that its tombstone is erect seems not to have been previously reported from folk tradition; neither has the idea of the tombstone that constantly falls over. A similar story is found in Hans Holzer, *Best True Ghost Stories* (Englewood Cliffs, New Jersey: Prentice-hall, Inc., 1983), pp. 44-46, concerning a Connecticut woman named Betty Tylaska. Her great-great-grandfather haunted her house until she discovered his tombstone in the basement and set it properly in a cemetery. There is also a tradition concerning the victims of the West Plains, Missouri, explosion of 1928 that says their tombstone constantly shifts (there were many unidentified victims who were buried in a common grave).

5. Collected December, 1964, by Mary Scott from Pedro Lujan in El Paso, Texas. The informant was a twenty-two year old student at Texas Western College (now the University of Texas at El Paso) who, apparently, told the story for entertainment. He did not recall where he heard the tale or from whom. The legend, however, is well known in Texas and has been around for some time. Its first published report came in 1937 in Charles L. Sonnichsen's article, "Mexican Spooks from El Paso," pp. 120-129 in volume 13, *Publications of the Texas Folklore Society* (Austin: Texas Folklore Society, 1937). According to Sonnichsen the ghost is of one Don Mauro Lujan and the house has been around since the 1870s. Sonnichsen's version contains several elements not mentioned by Pedro Lujan, including a buried treasure whose location is revealed to the family by the ghost. There are also more details about the relationship between the husband and the ghost. It is said that when the husband comes home late he must ask the ghost's permission to get in bed with his wife.

Motifs include E281.0.3* "Ghost haunts house, damaging property or annoying inhabitants" and E281.3(b) "Ghost lays hand on girl awake in bed." There seems to be no motif number listed for the amorous ghost who pinches women, an act that seems mischievous rather than malicious. Witches and, in European tradition, fairies often resort to pinching but in those cases the deed is done as punishment of their victims; this doesn't seem to be true in Lujan's narrative.

6. Collected in 1962 by Jan Calhoon from Dale Pope of Warren, Arkansas. Pope was the son of a farmer who lived near Warren all of his life. Apparently he didn't believe the tradition because it is related as a tradition held by others. For him, seemingly, it was just a good story. Motifs are D1003 "Magic blood—human" and E337.1.1 "Murder sounds heard just as they must have happened at time of death."

7. Collected October 31, 1982, by Jane Watson from Fran Franklin, Monticello, Arkansas. Mrs. Franklin is Assistant Professor of Speech at the University of Arkansas at Monticello where she is very popular with students. She firmly believes in ghosts and frequently relates this narrative, even using it in her classes, not only for entertainment but for other reasons as well. Watson, a former student, reflecting on the matter recalled, "It showed us, the students, a personal belief held by the instructor. It also worked to bind us together as a group, initiating free-flowing discussions between members of the class. These conversations almost always showed us another facet of one another." That a well-educated and respected person like Mrs. Franklin told a ghost story as truth also produced some perhaps-to-be-expected side effects. Watson notes, "One lovely lady from Star City, Arkansas, who is near seventy years old, was quite surprised that someone like Mrs. Franklin believed in ghosts. This discovery led her to blushingly tell the legend of her own about a ghost that inhabited their old home."

Motifs include E281 "Ghosts haunt house"; E334.4 "Ghost of suicide seen at death spot or near by"; E338(e) "Female ghost ascends, descends stairs"; E402.1.2 "Footsteps of invisible ghost heard"; and E402.1.3 "Invisible ghost plays musical instrument." Most of these motifs were first reported from oral tradition in the early 1800s but are much older.

8. Collected by Lewis David Bandy in 1940 from an unnamed white informant who also contributed the other haunted bed story in this volume, Text 51. Evidently, the narrator believed in the veracity of his story, but it also served an entertainment function. There is a sense conveyed that he was somewhat proud of having such an interesting and unusual experience to tell listeners. He was also a person who fancied himself somewhat daring and adventurous as attested to by his attempts to outdo whatever unseen force controlled the bed in the "back room." The use of words like "wham" and "kerpoodle" sound somewhat literary but not unlike the sort of language that might be used by a person who is histrionic.

Motifs here are E279.2 "Ghost disturbs sleeping person"; E279.3 "Ghost pulls bed-clothing from sleeper," a motif that is well-known in the folk tradition of both the British Isles and the United States; E281.3 "Ghost haunts particular room in house"; E421.1 "Invisible ghosts"; F1411 "Fear test: staying in haunted house"; and Thompson's H1376.2 "Quest: learning what fear is." In its general tenor this text bears some similarity to Type 376 "The Youth Who Wanted to Learn What Fear Is" in which a youth sets out to find fear, something of which he is ignorant. He tries several frightful experiences such as playing cards with the devil in church, stealing clothes from a ghost, staying at night in a cemetery or a haunted house, playing ninepins with a reassembled dead man, or being shaved by a ghostly barber.

9. Collected by Caroline McQueen Rhea in 1932 from a Mrs. Liddy (probably Lydia) Potter near Mountain City, Tennessee. She was apparently responding to a question, for her opening sentence is definitely not studied, but responsorial. Her very active participation in the story indicates that it is one she deeply believes. Her concluding remark "Hit's sin, jist sin, that's caused hit all" reveals that the legend also conveys a religious meaning to her. It seems likely, though, that it also functions in a sense as entertainment since it is a vividly recalled unusual series of incidents.

Motifs E422.1.11.5.1 "Ineradicable bloodstain after bloody tragedy" and E422.1.11.5.1(a) "Ineradicable bloodstain in stone or wood floor after bloody tragedy at spot" are applicable here although, as Mrs. Potter indicates, it is unclear just what happened to cause the stain. The motif is quite old in folk tradition and common in Denmark, the British Isles, and the United States. Other motifs found here include E574 "Appearance of ghost serves as death omen"; and the following two listed only in Thompson: D1812.5.1.12.2 "Bird calls as evil omen" and E714.1 "Soul (life) in the blood." Bird calls as an evil omen crops up in Korean folk narratives but is relatively uncommon in American tales. There is, however, a variety of folk beliefs common in the United States concerning owls and raincrows. One holds that a dog's howling portends death, especially when preceded by an owl hooting. Another says that merely seeing an owl, particularly at night, is a sign of impending death. Sometimes it is the color of the owl that is important, white and red owls being particularly bad omens. According to some accounts death results only if you are the only one to hear the owl's hoot. The raincrow, or cuckoo, is widely regarded as a sign of rain but rarely as an indicator of imminent death. Perhaps the key to understanding this aspect of folklore about the raincrow is contained in a Slovenian folksong which speaks of a treasonous act committed by a cuckoo, as a result of which Jesus was captured by his enemies. As a result the bird was punished by being made a harbinger of doom.

10. Collected November 19, 1976, by Anna Farrier from Elizabeth E. Apple, Huff, Arkansas. Mrs. Apple is well-known in her community not only as a narrator of interesting tales but also as a singer of old-time songs. She had most of her tales from her father who is probably the source of the narrative given here although that is not so indicated by Farrier. Apple has also made a concerted effort to gather interesting stories about local happenings and, as postmistress at Huff for several years, she acquired without much effort many such narratives from people picking up their mail. As the beginning of this test indicates, this tale was recorded during a session at which Mrs. Apple contributed several narratives, most of which dealt with the supernatural.

Motifs are E281 "Ghosts haunt house"; E402 "Mysterious ghostlike noises heard"; E402.1.5. "Invisible ghost makes rapping or knocking noise"; E402.1.2. "Footsteps of invisible ghost heard"; E421.1 "invisible ghosts"; and E451.8(c) "Ghost laid when house it haunts is burned."

11. Collected by William E. Lightfoot from Daisy Branham Banks, June 30, 1974, at her home on Jane Brown Branch near Prestonsburg, Kentucky. Mrs. Banks was born in Floyd County, Kentucky, in 1881 and lived in the area all of her life. She knew a good deal of supernatural lore and gave Lightfoot stories about witchcraft and of markings caused by fright in addition to this personal experience regarding a haunted house. Yet, despite this fund of material, she was no believer in all of these things. Speaking of witches she remarked, "Yeah, the people believed in them. I never did, but people did believe in them." She was less skeptical about marking, recalling that she had "been awful bad scared once that one of mine would be marked, but they wasn't, I made sure they wasn't marked." She did this by making up her mind not to be scared by any frightening that that happened to her while she was pregnant. The opening line of the story given here indicates her attitude towards ghosts and revenants. This sentence also suggests that Banks regarded herself as an open-minded, somewhat fearless person; this feeling is perhaps the main reason she tells the tale.

The major motif here is E281.0.3* "Ghosts haunt house, damaging property or annoying inhabitants," which is usually a puzzling narrative element because it is very difficult to tell whether the haunters are ghosts, witches, or familiar spirits, precisely the problem here. Other motifs are E338.1(aa) "Ghosts knock on door"; E421.1 "Invisible ghosts"; and E599.6 "Ghosts move furniture and household articles."

12. Collected November 7, 1975, by Lloyd Thornton from an unnamed fifty-eight year old white housewife in Jonesboro, Arkansas. The story was one that had been told to her by her father nearly fifty years earlier in her hometown of Lorado, Arkansas. The "back then" referred to in the first line of the story is a reference to some indeterminate time twenty-five to fifty years prior to the time she was told the story—that is, approximately one hundred years before Thornton recorded this text. This was one of many ghost stories told by her father and, apparently, the informant saw this solely as entertainment. She noted that her father's stories took the place of radios and television which, in the mid 1920s, were nonexistent in Lorado. She also frequently referred to the narrative as a legend, an almost certain indication that she did not believe the story to be true.

This sounds remarkably like a märchen but a search through Stith Thompson's *The Types of the Folktale* fails to turn up any exact parallel. Motifs include E281 "Ghosts haunt house"; E281.0.1 "Ghost kills man who stays in haunted house"; E402.1.1. "Vocal sounds of ghost of human being"; E545 "The dead speak"; and Thompson's E545.1 "Conversation between the dead."

13. Collected in 1964 by Jacqueline Miller from Mrs. William Ramsey, a housewife in El Paso, Texas. No other information is offered about Mrs. Ramsey so it is hard to determine her attitude toward the story or how she used it. Clearly the woman was a skillful narrator, indicated by the extensive dialogue and the general manner of presentation, and had probably related this legend several times.

Motifs include E322 "Dead wife's friendly return" and E415.4 "Dead cannot rest until money debts are paid."

14. Collected September 3, 1965, by George Foss from Mary Woods Shiflett, Browns Cove, Virginia. Mrs. Shiflett was born in 1902 and, at the time of collection, had been widowed for several years. A very energetic person, she supported herself, until illness confined her to a Baltimore nursing home, by cutting timber, running moonshine stills, making quilts, making apple butter, and housing up to a dozen welfare children at a time as foster parent. Since the story is related as a personal experience it may be told partly as proof of the existence of ghosts, but it also has a significant entertainment function. Shiflett's statement, "I could just set and talk all night about them ghost tales" indicates a considerable pride in having unusual experiences to relate.

Motifs include E402 "Mysterious ghostlike noises heard"; and E723.7.3 "Wraith opens and closes door." A very similar story from Alabama is given in Browne, *"A Night With the Hants,"* pp. 220-223.

15. Collected in 1967 by Pat Simons from Connie Herrera in El Paso, Texas. Miss Herrera also told the legend about the devil who appeared at the dance at Thomas Jefferson High School in El Paso (Text 74d), and more information about her is contained in the notes for that text. Since the story is related as a personal experience it is obvious that Herrera considers it more than just an entertaining story although it probably is related by her for that reason as well.

Motifs include E281.3(b) "Ghost lays hand on girl awake in bed" and E402.1.2 "Footsteps of invisible ghost heard."

16. Collected by Morris Emison, December 8, 1974, from her twenty-seven year old sister in Blytheville, Arkansas. The informant is a high school speech and drama teacher who taught for two years in Kansas but, at the time of the interview, worked in Blytheville. She digresses briefly to offer a theory about how legends originate, an action that makes it clear she does not believe the legend is factual. This view is already evident from her use of the term *legend*, a word rarely used to describe anything one believes. Actually, she only summarizes the legend, suggesting that she is a passive narrator for whom the story serves no function beyond entertainment. This latter view is enunciated by the informant who said, "This story, like the others I will tell you, would probably be told when a bunch of people get together and tell ghost stories and the like." The other stories she told were mostly ghost legends although she did tell a local character anecdote and a humorous story.

Motifs are E281 "Ghosts haunt house"; E310 "Dead lover's friendly return"; and J1782.3 "House noises thought to be ghosts."

17. Collected in Jonesboro, Arkansas, November 20, 1974, by Katherine Lemay from a twenty-year-old female college student from Ida, Arkansas, who is identified only as Carrie Ann. The informant is skeptical but not ready to call the story false. When asked if she believed the story she answered. "I'm not sure. I can't say no because my Mom would not lie, but I've never seen anything of the sort." Clearly, then, she sees it mainly as an entertaining, albeit unusual, story and, to some extent, so do her parents although they also believe they are providing a factual narrative. The informant told Lemay that her parents were recently talking about the house when "they were entertaining some friends. One of the women is super superstitious." The last sentence suggests the possibility that the informant might believe more deeply if she were not afraid of being called "super superstitious."

B546 "Animal searches for dead man" and E402.1.2 "Footsteps of invisible ghost heard," a motif frequently reported since the early 1800s, apply here.

18. Collected in Jonesboro, Arkansas, November 23, 1974, by Katherine Lemay from a nineteen-year-old female college student from Hope, Arkansas, who is not identified by name. Apparently, the story is mainly utilized by the girl for entertainment as the occasion for telling it was a rainy night in a college dormitory where several girls were telling ghost stories in a darkened room. She is, however, not entirely sure that the incident couldn't have happened and is therefore a bit leery about her marriage starting off with a supernatural experience like that encountered by her parents as newlyweds. The motif here is E279.3 "Ghost pulls bed clothing from sleeper," one with a long history and many published examples. For another story about a ghost who tampers with bed clothing that ends differently see Holzer, *Best True Ghost Stories,* pp. 77-79.

19. Collected by Ethel M. Cottingham and Travis Jordan from John L. Masten. No date or place of collection are given but it was recorded for the WPA in the mid-1930s and, based on the setting of the story, probably was collected in Forsyth County, North Carolina. The text has a very literary quality, noticeable even in the opening paragraph which contains descriptive words that would rarely be used in oral passages. There are, of course, some people who speak in such stilted language but there is good reason to believe that this text is the result of improvement," either by Cottingham or Jordan or by some other unnamed party. The best evidence for this suspicion is the nature of much WPA folklore collecting, which was done for the purpose of gathering material that could be used for literary transmission. In many states the tests gathered were rewritten rather than presented in the exact words of informants. Since only Masten's name is given it is impossible to determine exactly what function this narrative served for the informant. Because the collectors were, in most instances, concerned with getting tales that were interesting and entertaining it is probably reasonable to assume that Masten found the story entertaining. It also undoubtedly offered an interesting explanation for some unusual and mysterious noises.

Motifs include E402.1.1.3 "Ghost cries and screams"; and Thompson's P214.1 "Wife commits suicide (dies) on death of husband"; and T86.3 "Mistress springs into dead lover's grave."

20. Collected October 14, 1976, by Anna Farrier from Elizabeth E. Apple, Huff, Arkansas. For more information about Apple see the notes for Text 10, collected by Farrier from her. Mrs. Apple had this tale from her father, and several others in her repertoire are from the same source. Evidently this, and other narratives she related, were both entertaining to her and regarded as part of local history.

The word *jayhawker* originally applied to a group of anti-slavery guerrilla fighters on the Kansas-Missouri border that was later incorporated into the Union army. This group was notorious for their burnings and killings. Eventually Confederate propagandists branded all Union sentiment in Arkansas as the work of jayhawkers. History books today generally refer to Union raiders as jayhawkers and Confederate raiders as bushwackers. Ozarkers make no such careful distinctions; to them all guerrillas who specialized in terrorizing those left at home during the war are usually labeled jayhawkers. Most informants still regard these persons as thugs or deserters or worse who were taking advantage of the Civil War to line their own pockets. Narratives about jayhawkers are still commonly encountered throughout the Ozarks. For a discussion of some of these see James J. Johnston's, "Jayhawker Stories: Historical Lore in the Arkansas Ozarks," *Mid-South Folklore* IV:1 (Spring, 1976), pp.3-9.

In some folk traditions there is a taboo against taking down the body of a hanged man, but of course, that is not why the people in this narrative were afraid to take the boy's corpse down. Their only worry was the jayhawkers who might return and kill them. Motifs are E274 "Gallows ghost"; E274(a) "Ghost haunts scene of unjust execution"; and E530.1 "Ghost-like lights."

21. Collected 1961 by Ruthann Luedicke from Ruth Henderson Martin of Hot Springs, Arkansas, who had the story from her grandparents. Evidently, Martin viewed the narrative as a bit of family history as well as just an interesting, unusual story. The battle at Pleasant Hill, Louisiana, took place April 9, 1864 and, contrary to Martin's text, was far from being one of the last Civil War battles in Louisiana.

Motifs include E235.4.6(a) "Theft of teeth punished by scare from ghost who returns, takes teeth," a motif primarily found in Afro-American legendry; E328* "Dead returns for something forgotten"; E338(a) "Male ghost seen"; E338.1(b) "Ghost looks in at window"; E421.2.1 "Ghost leaves no footprints"; and E422.1.11.2 "Revenant as face or head." The second ghost here, like those in several American narratives, seems to have returned for no specific purpose. For more on this aspect of ghostly behavior see Louis M. Jones, *Three Eyes on the Past: Exploring New York Folk Life* (Syracuse: Syracuse University Press, 1982), pp. 35-59, especially see pp. 46-49. the "dogtrot" mentioned here refers to a specific type of architecture that developed in the United States about 1825. Dogtrot houses are one-story buildings composed of two equal units separated by a broad open central hall and joined by a common roof. The term probably arose as a colorful description of the open central hall as a place where dogs could trot through at their own leisure.

22. Collected in 1962 by Jan Calhoon from Dale Pope of Warren, Arkansas. More information about Pope is given in the notes to Text 6. There were two reported Civil War engagements at Mark's Mills, one a skirmish on April 5, 1864, and the second the battle on April 25 of that year. According to Col. John M. Harrell in *Confederate Military History*, X (New York: Thomas Yoseloff, 1962; reprint of a work originally issued in 1899), p. 260, "this engagement took place in a forest of pines not far from the west bank of the Saline River, in a spot usually lonely and undisturbed by any sound ruder than the winds in the treetops." The battle lasted approximately four hours, and losses were quite heavy for such a relatively short battle, casualties numbering close to a thousand. So the engagement at Mark's Mills was a "small battle" only in the amount of time it lasted, not in the loss of lives involved.

Motifs include E334.5 "Ghost of soldier haunts battlefield"; E402 "Mysterious ghost-like noises heard"; E402.1.1.2 "Ghost moans"; and E410 "The unquiet grave."

23. Collected in 1932 by Caroline McQueen Rhea from Dave Greer near Mountain City, Tennessee. Greer was a member of a pioneer Tennessee family and apparently knew several ghost legends, of which he told Rhea at least two (see notes to Text 30). Even so, he was not a particularly skillful narrator, for his texts are basically summaries. Probably they were told primarily for entertainment which, if so, makes the lack of dialogue a major deficiency. Moreover, there is a literary sound to this text since some of the language is not typical of that usually given in oral narratives. Nevertheless, his descriptive passages do provide a dramatic backdrop for the story, placing the setting in a heavily forested, secluded region that has been haunted since the Civil War. The sense of drama continues through the yarn for the murderer was never identified. Neither was the reason for Mrs. Songo's suicide ever discovered. But, while these features provide interest in the story they also leave an essentially incomplete tale, one with no denouement.

Motifs are E275 "Ghost haunts place of great accident or misfortune"; E337.1.1 "Murder sounds heard just as they must have happened at time of death"; E402.1.1.3 "Ghost cries and screams"; K910 "Murder by strategy"; and several given only by Thompson. These are the general motif K950 "Various kinds of treacherous murder"; and the more specialized K959.4 "Murder from behind"; P201.1 "Feud between two branches of family"; and P214.1 "Wife commits suicide on death of husband."

24. Collected by Caroline McQueen Rhea in 1932 from Mrs. W.C. Wright of Silver Lake, Tennessee. Actually, Mrs. Wright did not relate the story but wrote it out, presumably because she was somewhat shy about telling the narrative to Rhea. This suggests that she was not a person who ordinarily related legends, at least not to strangers. In short, she was a passive narrator of this type of lore. The text she provides is etiological; that is, it explains the origin of a somewhat unusual place name. While such explication is Wright's main purpose she also seems to view the yarn as entertaining.

Motifs here are E402 "Mysterious ghostlike noises heard"; E402.1.1.2 "Ghost moans"; E411 "Dead cannot rest because of a sin," a motif that is rarely encountered in America although it is well-known in the British Isles; and three cited only by Thompson. These are S100 "Revolting murders or mutilations"; S110.5 "Murderer kills all who come to certain spot"; and S180 "Wounding or torturing." Surprisingly, neither Thompson nor Baughman gives a motif number for a feud between two families which is one of the most distinctive features of this narrative. For more about the Bloody Third and the Jingling Hole see the first text in Section 4 of this book.

25. Collected August 4, 1977, by William E. Lightfoot from Joe T. Fletcher, a farmer near Waterloo, Georgia. Fletcher was born in 1905 and has earned his living as a farmer since 1935. Mr. Fletcher knew a number of legends and anecdotes that he related to Lightfoot. The words he uses in this text make it evident that he is not really a believer in the supernatural disappearance of the mill. He calls it "the biggest story I ever heard" and emphasizes that "I've never knowed that to be a fact," further noting that "they" said it happened. All of these things suggest that the story functions for him partly as entertainment and partly as a bit of local history. Lightfoot collected another version of the Crystal/Bone Lake legend from a Carlos Ross of Sycamore, Georgia, who claimed that the supernatural disappearance was just fiction. According to him, what really happened was that "the water riz up on the old gristmill. And they finally moved it, I guess, sold it for junk, the people did. After he was hung."

Relevant motifs here include F713.2 "Bottomless lakes (pools)"; F940 "Extraordinary underground (underwater) disappearance"; and Thompson's D910 "Magic body of water." The term "open range" refers to a time when grazing grounds were not fenced off and, thus, open to anyone's cattle. This condition no longer exists in Georgia or in most other states.

26. Reported 1959 by Drew Velvin from Lewisville, Arkansas, but his source is not named; Velvin himself is possibly the informant. There is a reportorial quality about the text ("Many are scared," "many say," etc.) suggesting that the story is mainly entertainment for the narrator. The opening in mythological times is a nice touch, especially when contrasted with the immediately following passage bringing the story down to contemporary times. This indicates that the person has some experience in relating stories designed to hold audience attention.

Motifs are E530.1 "Ghost-like lights" and E599.7 "Ghost carries lantern." Spirit Lake is located about four miles from Lewisville.

27. Collected by Robert Mason in 1939 from his grandmother in Cannon County, Tennessee. The tale was a favorite entertainment in Mason's family, particularly on windy and rainy nights which created an appropriate atmosphere. Repeated retellings, and the entertainment function, perhaps account for the somewhat literary descriptive passages used in this text. Sections like "a delegation of them would voluntarily go into the graveyard at the side of the hill without male escort" are certainly more typical of a carefully rehearsed written account than of a spontaneous oral text.

This tale is a widely known type classified in Stith Thompson's, *The Types of the Folktale* (Helsinki: Folklore Fellows Communications, 1964), p. 475, as 1676B "Clothing caught in graveyard." Known in Finland, Sweden, Holland, Iraq, Italy, Hungary, England, and the United States, it has been collected by various folklorists for almost a century and was most likely around for a long time before any collections were made. The Tennessee text differs from most versions in that the girls visit the graveyard in a group rather then singly. In addition, they stick forks into the graves rather than stakes. Although quite old, the story is still very popular; I have collected versions in Arkansas in the past three years and know from other folklorists that it is well-known in other parts of the United States. Baughman lists this both as a tale type and as motif N384.2(a) "Person goes to cemetery on a dare: he is to plant a stake in a grave or stick a knife or fork or sword or nail into a grave (or coffin). The knife is driven through the person's loose cuff, or the nail is driven through part of the sleeve, or the stake is driven through the person's long coat tail."

Other motifs here are Thompson's F1041.1.11 "Death from fear" and H1416 "Fear test: spending night by grave."

28. Collected by W.K. McNeil from Ella Fletcher of Onia, Arkansas, April 14, 1981. Mrs. Fletcher was born in 1907 and is a firm believer in ghosts and tells this, and some other ghost stories involving various members of her family, as evidence that ghosts do indeed exist. She was being interviewed about local history and, when asked about any unusual events that had happened in the community, brought up the subject of ghosts and proceeded to tell this story about her father. The incident described here happened near a famous house in the community of Onia that is now called the Uncle Bud Moore House. Built in the 1890s and burned down in the 1960s, the Bud Moore House is well-known in Onia as the scene of a number of unusual happenings. At one time Mrs. Fletcher lived in the house and told me about some of the supernatural things that occurred while she was a resident. One such incident that especially impressed her involved her daughter. In Mrs. Fletcher's words: "People told us before we moved there, they said, 'You won't stay there, you'll see things and get scared.' Well, my daughter, well, she went out on a date one night, and when any of the kids were out I couldn't go to sleep until they came home. Well, she come home and didn't make no racket and shut the doors, and I didn't hear her come home. Well, her bedroom was there in the back corner and she had come in and got undressed and went to bed. Well, her door to her bedroom kinda drug on the floor when it was shut and it was hard to shut. Well, along in the night, I'd say about ten, I heard this door drag like someone was shutting it. Well, next morning I got up and went down and was making breakfast and my daughter came down in her gown in the kitchen and said, 'Mama, I heard something last night.'

"I asked her what time she got in last night and she said, 'About nine.' Well, I heard that door drag and she said she heard it too. It was something, it was! Now, I was across the hall and I heard it."

Motifs involved here are E281 "Ghosts haunt house" and E402.1 "Noises presumably caused by ghost of person." The relevant motifs in her story about her father are E332.1 "Ghost appears at road and stream"; E332.2 "Person meets ghost on road"; and E332.2(h) "Ghost seen on road at night." When Mrs. Fletcher says that the man "just lit up" she does not mean that there was a luminescence about him but merely that he got up.

29a and b The first text was collected November 10, 1974, by Janet Thomasson in Jonesboro, Arkansas, from an unnamed white female informant who, at the time of the collection, was forty-four years old. The informant grew up fifteen miles from the scene of the story and first heard about the face in the window from her grandmother. As her concluding words indicate, she is not quite ready to refute the legend but is well aware of its publicity value. She told Thomasson that "when we had visitors from out of state, we always drove down to Carrollton to show them the face on the window." She added that "it looks almost like a negative rather than a picture, its eyes, nose and mouth, but it's like an oil slick on water." For the informant, then, the main function the legend serves is entertainment, but it does have some broader implications. For the citizens of Carrollton it provides a graphic reminder of the pitfalls of hasty judgment, as a result of which an innocent man was executed. The legend also gives the town a "claim to fame" and an illustration of the idea of divine retribution, that is, those who punish will be punished.

The second text was collected in 1975 by Jim Harkins from his father, Jim Harkins, Sr., now living in Oklahoma City but a native of Aliceville. Although similar to the Carrollton legend this one about Aliceville is not exactly the same. Since the two towns are located only about fifteen miles apart it would be interesting to know if two traditions have been blended together here. An interesting difference is that the race of the innocently executed man is not mentioned in the second tale. Probably the Aliceville legend serves essentially the same functions as the Carrollton one.

Motifs here are E532 "Ghost-like picture" and E532(a) "Ghost-like portrait etched in glass."

30. Collected by Caroline McQueen Rhea in 1932 from Dave Greer near Mountain City, Tennessee. Greer also related the legend about Songo Hollow (Text 23), and more information about him is given there. This tale explaining the origin of a place name doesn't sound so literary as the one dealing with Songo Hollow. While explanation is certainly the main point of the narrative, the structure and method of presentation suggest that entertainment is also one of its most important functions. There is little intrusion of the narrator in the story, much character delineation, and an ordering of events with a specific time slot for each.

Motifs are E402.1.3 "Invisible ghost plays musical instrument"; E402.1.3(a) "Ghost plays violin"; and four given only in Thompson. These are A1617 "Origin of place-name";

D1233 "Magic violin (fiddle)"; D1441.1.3 "Magic fiddle calls animals together"; and Z355 "All snakes but one placated by music."

31. Collected November 2, 1982 by Stacy VanAusdall from Faye Newsome in Harrisburg, Arkansas. At the time of the interview Newsome was sixty years old, meaning that she was born in 1921 or 1922. Mrs. Newsome, who worked in the home of the collector's family, is said to have "extensive knowledge of everyone in the small town of Harrisburg (1984 population, 1,910)" and particularly of the Negro community there. Apparently, she is also a skillful narrator for the collector notes, "Faye's style and method of telling it very deliberate and precise. She sat very relaxed with her hands folded in her lap while she told the story she has undoubtedly told many times before. She speaks very quietly and pauses a great deal for dramatic effect." Her skill, however, is mainly in the manner of telling, not in the text, which is essentially a summary of the legend. The last paragraph makes it clear that Newsome believes the story but, within the Negro community of Harrisburg, it probably serves many functions. First, it is a moralistic temperance narrative in which a drunkard drives his wife and, ultimately, himself to the grave, but even in death their souls can't rest. Presumably others inclined to partake of alcohol should beware lest they find the same fate. Second, it provides an explanation for some unusual noises that have apparently been heard by many people. It, then, is entertainment, a story proving the existence of ghosts, a temperance yarn, and an explanatory tale.

Motifs include E273 "Churchyard ghosts"; E401 "Voices of dead heard from graveyard"; E402 "Mysterious ghostlike noises heard"; E402.1.1.2 "Ghost moans"; E402.1.1.3 "Ghost cries and screams"; and E410 "The unquiet grave."

32a and b Both versions collected by Johnny Lloyd Redd, the first in June, 1976, from Linda Sue Redd Harris and the second, also in June, 1976, from Jess Seawell. The first text was recorded in Jonesboro, Arkansas, while the second was recorded in Maynard, Arkansas. Harris was a twenty-six year old secretary who, at the time of the collection, lived in Jonesboro but until she graduated from high school lived in Stokes, Arkansas, where she heard much conversation concerning Ashberry "Rip" Sago. Seawell, a seventy-three year old retiree at the time of collection, knew Sago as a young man. Although one informant knew the old coffinmaker personally, both tell the legend essentially for entertainment. Seawell's last line indicates, however, that he also uses it as a kind of exemplum predicting a terrible end for kids who are not good.

Motifs include D1856 "Death evaded"; E354* "Dead returns to complete task"; E363.3(c) "Ghost warns of approaching storm"; E378* "Ghost continues to remain in usual surroundings after death"; E402 "Mysterious ghostlike noises heard"; E402.3 "Sound made by ghostly object"; and E419.8 "Ghost returns to enforce its burial wishes or to protest disregard of such wishes."

33. Collected by Gilbert Cooley in 1974 from an unnamed back male from Dillon, South Carolina. Cooley also collected an almost identical story from another informant from Rowland, North Carolina. Since it is related as a personal experience the informant clearly believes the story and, possibly, tells the tale as proof of the existence of ghosts. This is a version of a well-known legend called by folklorists "The Baby with the Fangs" and is primarily associated with Mexicans and Mexican-Americans. It is also known in Cuba and Bolivia and possibly other Latin American countries. Unlike Cooley's text, most versions indicate that the baby is a witch or the devil. Typically the legend has a man traveling at night, either on horseback, driving a car, or walking. He finds the baby beside the road, lying on a grave behind a tombstone, in a barn, or under a bridge. He picks the child up and carries it off. The baby soon starts to grow, rapidly becoming too heavy to carry, turns into a witch, develops unusually long, sharp teeth or fangs, grows long sharp nails, horns and tail. The man drops the child or it simply disappears.

Few versions of this legend are related as personal experiences. Possibly Cooley's informant merely told the story as a personal experience to heighten the dramatic effect. Motifs are Thompson's D55.2.5 "Transformation: adult to child"; D56 "Magic change in person's age"; and D56.1 "Transformation to older person."

34. Collected Summer, 1974, by Pat Blake from an unnamed twenty-six year old male computer operator in Jonesboro, Arkansas. Clearly the informant believes the story since it describes a personal experience but he also sees it as entertainment and is somewhat proud of having such an unusual experience. He told Blake, "I can remember telling it to friends when we were telling ghost stories, and when we traded stories about weird things that had happened to us." To the many others who told about the bugler and his horse the legend probably served some other purposes. By emphasizing this supernatural event that occurs in a cemetery after dark, youths were hopefully discouraged from loitering in graveyards after nightfall. The story can also be seen as a comment on the loyalty of animals. Like many other supernatural occurrences this one is said to happen usually when there is a full moon.

Motifs are E520 "Animal ghosts" and 521.1 "Ghost of horse."

35. Collected March 12, 1977, by Eric Batchelder from Oma Little in Paint Rock, Alabama. Mrs. Little told Batchelder a number of supernatural stories but considered this the most unique, perhaps because it was a personal experience. Actually, this account of the haunted hollow is not a story so much as it is a series of related incidents. Motifs are E338.1(c) "Ghost opens doors and windows repeatedly"; E402 "Mysterious ghostlike noises heard"; E402.2 "Sounds made by invisible ghosts of animals"; E421.1 "Invisible ghosts"; and E530.1 "Ghost-like lights."

36. Collected December 8, 1974, by Morris Emison from her sister in Blytheville, Arkansas. For more information about this informant see the notes to Text 16 in Section 1 of this book, which concerns H. L. Hunt's house in El Dorado, Arkansas. This legend functions as entertainment for the informant but probably it also serves to create a feeling of unity and tradition among the student body of Henderson State University. In short, the Black Lady represents the school spirit (pun intended). OBU is Ouachita Baptist University.

Motifs include E230 "Return from dead to inflict punishment"; E411.1.1 "Suicide cannot rest in grave"; and Thompson's T81.2.2 "Scorned lover kills self."

37. Collected in 1983 by Jill Pimentall and Craig O'Dell from Kathy Jones, Gaston, South Carolina. Since the story is told as a personal experience, the informant obviously believes the story is a factual account. Even so, she still finds it hard to believe in ghosts but, clearly, she enjoys telling this tale. She told the collectors that she had related this story two hundred times. The ghost is supposed to be of George I. Pair (1924-1962), the first principal of Airport High which, at the time of its construction in 1958, was the second high school in the Cayce-West Columbia, South Carolina area. The Mr. Rivers mentioned by Jones is Ed Rivers, custodian at the school and a close friend of Pair's, who has reported seeing the ghost several times. The incident described constitutes Jone's only encounter with the apparition.

Although Jones sees the narrative mainly as an eerie personal experience validating the existence of ghosts, the numerous reports of sightings by others possibly serve a broader, more useful function. Would-be vandals may be scared away by stories of the school's supernatural "guardian." There is also a sense of pride in stories about the ghost for he gives Airport High a distinction that no other schools in the area have, their very own resident wraith. This feeling is particularly conveyed in an article titled "School Spirit Haunts Halls of Airport" that appeared in the Monday, October 31, 1983, issue of a local paper, *The Eyrie.* In an almost bragging manner the author of the article asks, "But did you know that Airport has its own resident ghost?" and proceeds to describe some encounters that faculty members have had with the spirit of the former principal. For whatever the reasons the legend is perpetuated, it is certain that those who pass it on believe in the reality of Pair's ghost. From evidence presented by the collectors it seems to be taken very seriously by both students and faculty members. Most persons who have sighted the apparition are convinced he is there to protect the school which, reportedly, he loved above everything except his family. One informant voiced this opinion succinctly when he said, "I always wind up by telling people that he is not going to hurt you unless you are trying to do something to hurt the school."

Motifs are E300 "Friendly return from the dead"; E330 "Locations haunted by the non-malevolent dead"; E422.4.5 "Revenant in male dress"; and E425 "Revenant in human form."

38. Collected in 1938 by Henry Wacaster Perry from Orpha Harrison, a white woman living in Carter County, Tennessee. She heard it from her sister-in-law, who had learned it from her grandfather. That it is a story the grandfather "used to tell" and, that it is about one of her uncles suggest that it was used in the family as an object lesson. This is also indicated by the missionary-like ending that emphasizes, "This never left until this sinful man fell on his knees and began to pray. After that he was never bothered any more, for he became a religious man." It seems likely, though, that the narrative functions as entertainment also.

Motifs utilized here include E421.2.1 "Ghost leaves no footprints," a motif common in English, Canadian, and American folk tradition but first reported from England in 1850; G303.3.1 "The devil in human form"; G303.3.1.21 "The devil as a great hairy man"; and three cited only by Thompson, S60 "Cruel spouse"; S62 "Cruel husband"; and V254.4 "Devil exorcised by 'Ave.'" The Tennessee text bears some similarity to Thompson's type 760 "The Unquiet Grave" in which a man burns his three wives but can find no rest in the grave. A girl takes the dead man to a priest and secures his pardon for the murder of his wives. That type, of course, is a fictional tale whereas Harrison's narrative is told as an actual happening.

39. Collected in 1938 by Henry Wacaster Perry from John Harrison, an elderly white resident of Carter County, Tennessee. Like several other stories in this book, Harrison's is a reminiscence of a personal experience. In other words it is what folklorists call a *memorate* (pronounced "mem-o-rat"), a narrative of a personal happening usually involving the supernatural. Perry had heard the story numerous times prior to its recording one winter evening in 1938. Thus, the tale clearly serves an entertainment function but the narrator also believes this is actually what happened. His concluding line "Now, it looked to me like that was a warnin' or somethin'" shows just how seriously Harrison takes his story and why he frequently tells it. Just what the disease, double menthole, that claimed Butler's life is remains as much of a puzzle to me as it was to Harrison. Possibly the illness was something like pneumonia.

Motifs include D1812.5 "Future learned through omens," which is also a frequently encountered folk belief as well as a traditional narrative element; E574 "Appearance of ghost serves as death omen"; and two listed only by Thompson, E783.6 "Headless body vital" and M341.1.2 "Prophecy: early death." For both of these motifs Thompson cites an Irish myth as his only reference.

40. Collected by William E. Lightfoot from George Tucker on March 13, 1974 at Big Mud Creek near Beaver, Kentucky. Born November 6, 1917, Tucker is well known not only locally but nationally as a banjo player and he has appeared at numerous folk festivals and on several records. Evidently he believes in the events related in the tale for it is presented as a personal experience. It is unclear whether or not the opening is an indication that Tucker is proud of the story which is "something" or he is merely responding to a request from the collector to give him something of a supernatural nature. Tucker provides some dialogue and is a skillful taleteller, but, from a purely narrative standpoint, this text leaves something to be desired. We never learn what the host was after or why he is haunting this particular spot. In other words, like some other ghosts described in this book, he appears for no apparent reason.

The motifs here are E422.1.1(a) "Headless man—mention of appearance only" and Thompson's F511.0.1 "Headless person."

41. Collected by Andy Fulkerson in 1974 from Reese Hutcheson, a twenty-nine year old Episcopal priest in Paragould, Arkansas. Hutcheson received his theology degree in 1971 from the University of the South at Sewanee, Tennessee, and, at the time of collection, was parish priest for All Saints' Episcopal Church in Paragould. During the course of the interview, Hutcheson made it clear the legend was for him nothing more than entertainment, and it probably serves the same function for most students from the University of the South who discuss the topic. The typically rather uneventful college life can be made somewhat more exciting by a ghost. But even if Hutcheson had not expressed a certain skepticism toward the existence of the ghost, it would be evident from his text. The entire legend is told as if it is someone else's story that he is merely reporting. Such lines as "the legend goes," "supposed to have been seen by," "said to be," "said to," "reports come from someone who saw somebody, etc." are not words used by a narrator who deeply believes the story he is relating. Yet despite Hutcheson's skepticism, he commented that "still, some very weird noises come down those hallowed halls very early in the morning after having studied hours on end."

Probably the legend mainly serves a function of entertainment, and there is indeed something humorous about a person getting so much knowledge that his head falls off. The narrative can also be seen as an admonition not to put off studying until the last minute. Those who do not heed the warning run the risk of sharing the fate of the student who did so much cramming that his head fell off. Motifs are E422.1.1.5* "Miscellaneous actions of headless ghosts" and Thompson's D1641.7 "Severed head moves from place to place."

42. Collected in 1968 by Bill Ferris from Gene Autrey, a ten year old black boy in Leland, Mississippi. He also contributed the text about the ghost who turned his head backwards (Text 57). His attitude towards this text is indicated by the first sentence. The only relevant motif here is E422.1.1(a) "Headless man—mention of appearance only."

43. Collected by William E. Lightfoot and Tom Alder from Martin "Marty" Weathers of Glenville, Georgia, August 15, 1977. Weathers was a sophomore at Abraham Baldwin Agricultural College in Tifton where this text was recorded. He, and a friend from Barnesville, Georgia, named Bill Henry, contributed several legend and custom texts to Lightfoot even though they "were perpetually bewildered that 'college professors' were seriously interested in their customs and stories." Weathers was apparently an excellent informant, but the text given here is not especially distinguished as a narrative. Essentially it is just a summary of the legend; Weathers even seems uncertain about some of the essential details, such as why the girl had to stay late. Some of his wording indicates that for him the legend serves only an entertainment function. For example, he refers to it as a kind of "garbage," hardly the categorization that would be given by a believer.

The relevant motifs here are E275 "Ghost haunts place of great accident or misfortune"; D334 "Non-malevolent ghost haunts scene of former misfortune, crime, or tragedy"; E402 "Mysterious ghostlike noises heard"; and E402.1.1.3 "Ghost cries and screams." On August 10, 1977, five days before Lightfoot and Adler recorded this text, Lightfoot and Dave Stanley collected another version of the Omega Bridge legend from Teresa Lindsey, an employee of Abraham Baldwin Agricultural College. According to Mrs. Lindsey, "When I-75 was first built a woman, and I think two children, were riding down there and they were killed on that curve. And the noise that I guess your tires make from the curve is supposed to be the screams from her children as they died."

44. Collected August 30, 1965, by George Foss from Mary Woods Shiflett, Browns Cove, Virginia. For more information about Mrs. Shiflett see the notes to Text 14. Since the story here is told as a personal experience it is clearly related not just as entertainment. Probably Mrs. Shiflett told the story primarily as a testimony to the existence of ghosts.

The main motif here is E423.1.1 "Revenant as dog," but Thompson's F401.3.3 "Spirit as black dog" is also suggested. Browns Cove is just a few miles from the Skyline Drive of the Blue Ridge Parkway, a region that has a lengthy tradition of spectral black dogs. In the *Journal of American Folklore*, 20 (1907), pp. 151-152, a Mrs. R. F. Herrick, who mostly wrote articles on ballads, submitted the following information on "The Black Dog of the Blue Ridge":

In Botetourt County, Virginia, there is a pass that was much travelled by people going to Bedford County and by visitors to mineral springs in the vicinity. In the year 1683 the report was spread that at the wildest part of the trail in this pass there appeared at sunset a great black dog, who, with majestic tread, walked in a listening attitude about two hundred feet and then turned and walked back. Thus he passed back and forth like a sentinel on guard, always appearing at sunset to keep his nightly vigil and disappearing again at dawn. And so the whispering went with bated breath from one to another, until it had travelled from one end of the state to the other. Parties of young cavaliers were made up to watch for the black dog. Many saw him. Some believed him to be a veritable dog sent by some master to watch, others believed him to be a witch dog.

A party decided to go through the pass at night, well armed, to see if the dog would molest them. Choosing a night when the moon was full they mounted good horses and sallied forth. Each saw a great dog larger than any dog they had ever seen, and, clapping spurs to their horses, they rode forward. But they had not calculated on the fear of their steeds. When they approached the dog, the horses snorted with fear, and in spite of whip, spur, and rein gave him a wide berth, while he marched on as serenely as if no one were near. The party were unable to force their horses to take the pass again until after daylight. Then they were laughed at by their comrades to whom they told their experiences. Thereupon they decided to lie in ambush, kill the dog, and bring in his hide. The next night found the young men well hidden behind rocks and bushes with guns in hand. As the last ray of sunlight kissed the highest peak of the Blue ridge, the black dog appeared at the lower end of his walk and came majestically toward them. When he came opposite, every gun cracked. When the smoke cleared away, the great dog was turning at the end of his walk, seemingly unconscious of the presence of the hunters. Again and again they fired and still the dog walked his beat. And fear caught the hearts of the hunters, and they fled wildly away to their companions, and the black dog held the pass at night unmolested.

Time passed, and year after year went by, until seven years had come and gone, when a beautiful woman came over from the old country, trying to find her husband who eight years before had come to make a home for her in the new land. She traced him to Bedford County and from there all trace of him was lost. Many remembered the tall, handsome man and his dog. Then there came to her ear the tale of the vigil of the great dog of the mountain pass, and she pleaded with the people to take her to see him, saying that if he was her husband's dog he would know her. A party was made up and before night they arrived at the gap. The lady dismounted, and walked to the place where the nightly watch was kept. As the shadows grew long, the party fell back on the trail, leaving the lady alone, and as the sun sank into his purple bed of splendor the great dog appeared. Walking to the lady, he laid his great head in her lap for a moment, then turning he walked a short way from the trail, looking back to see that she was following. He led her until he paused by a large rock, where he gently scratched the ground, gave a long, low wail, and disappeared. The lady called the party to her and asked them to dig. As they had no implements, and she refused to leave, one of them rode back for help. When they dug below the surface they found the skeleton of a man and the hair and bones of a great dog. They found a seal ring on the hand of the man and a heraldic embroidery in silk that the wife recognized. She removed the bones for proper burial and returned to her old home. It was never known who had killed the man. But from that time to this the great dog, having finished his faithful work, has never appeared again.

Unlike the canine in Herrick's narrative the ghostly dog that appeared to Mrs. Shiflett was apparently motiveless.

45. Collected by William E. Lightfoot from Reuben Lowe, November 20, 1973, in Pikeville, Kentucky. Mr. Lowe, who was born in Pike County in 1909, is a retired coal miner who now earns his living as a farmer. He and his wife, Ruth, told Lightfoot a large number of supernatural tales concerning witches, burnstoppers, thrash (thrush) healers, measurers, magic healing, ghosts, and markings caused by fright and seemingly strongly believed in the validity of such traditions. In some cases, though, he had some difficulty recalling how the tradition worked. For example, in discussing a measurer (someone who cures a child's illness by measuring techniques) he commented: "What *we* always done was to measure a baby's length and to, to a ...I believe it was a sourwood tree...and cut a notch on it that high. And by the time it gets above that...something or other. I don't know. My wife knows. I just can't think of what happens here." Considering his degree of belief in the supernatural and his several personal experiences pertaining to ghostly things, it seems certain that he tells such stories as evidence of his belief and as testimony on behalf of such things as ghosts. Possibly, they also serve a secondary function such as entertainment. The town mentioned in the text is Pikeville, Kentucky, and the incident occurred circa 1927.

The only relevant motif here is E422.1.11.1 "Revenant as an eye" which has rarely been collected in folk tradition. The only previous reporting is in Charles M. Skinner's popular volume of 1903, *American Myths and Legends,* which consists of rewritten folk narratives. Unfortunately, Skinner does not identify his source but his text was set in Pennsylvania.

46. Collected by Caroline McQueen Rhea in 1932 from Mrs. Harrison Donnelly of Shouns, Tennessee. Apparently the tale was told primarily for entertainment; at least that's what its very structured arrangement suggests. If anything, it is a little too well ordered and reads more like a literary piece than an oral narrative. The impersonal sequential arrangement is typical of literary efforts as is some of the language utilized here. A reference to the ghost as an "invisible guest," to the doctor who "bounded forward" to meet the ghost, to his being "much disgruntled" and having "an unfortunate taste for drink," as well as several other phrases given here suggest a literary style rather than an oral one. There are, of course, some people who speak in such stilted language and Mrs. Donnelly may have been one. The net effect is that her use of euphemistic language suggests that she is both appalled and intrigued by the events she relates.

Motifs include E371.4 "Ghost of man returns to point out hidden treasure"; E402 "Mysterious ghost-like noises heard"; E421.1 "Invisible ghosts"; E421.2.1 "Ghost leaves no footprints," a motif first reported from England in 1850; and E451.8 "Ghost laid when house it haunts is destroyed or changed."

47. Collected June, 1973, by Michael O. Thomas from his aunt, Lee Thomas, in Kinston, North Carolina. The informant spent most of her childhood on farms in Lenoir and Greene counties, the latter being the county in which Snow Hill is located. Miss Thomas first heard this story as a young girl from a Mrs. Tillman, one of the daughters of the Mr. Jones in the narrative. The incident reportedly took place between 1910 and 1912, and at that time the house was old. Part of the room was sealed off because "the owner of the house had died of smallpox, and nobody wanted to handle his things." Miss Thomas said that Mr. Jones found "several thousand dollars" in the overcoat.

Motifs include E371 "Return from dead to reveal hidden treasure"; E402 "Mysterious ghostlike noises heard"; H1411 "Fear test: staying in haunted house"; and Thompson's E373.1 "Money received from ghosts as reward for bravery"; E436.2 "Cats crossing one's path sign of ghosts"; and E545.12 "Ghost directs man to hidden treasure."

48. Collected June, 1973, by Michael O. Thomas from his aunt, Lee Thomas, in Kinston, North Carolina. She heard this story when she was a young girl from a Mrs. Tillman who claimed to have had this encounter with a ghost. Reportedly, the incident took place on a farm near Hugo, North Carolina, in 1916 or 1917. This story, like the preceding text which was also told by Miss Thomas, was probably related by the informant mainly for entertainment but she was also aware that it was part of local history.

Motifs include E545.19.2 "Proper means of addressing ghost"; and Thompson's E373 "Ghosts bestow gifts on living" and E545.12 "Ghosts direct man to hidden treasure."

49. Collected in 1974 by Gilbert Cooley from an unnamed black male from Rowland, North Carolina. The informant had this story from his father who told him that "enchanted money" was money that was being guarded by a spirit. He told Cooley that during the Civil War the master would take a slave along with him when he was ready to bury some money. Once the money was in the ground the master would tell the slave to stay there and guard the treasure. Then, while the slave was obeying orders, he would be shot by the master so that the slave's spirit was left to guard the money. In this story, however, the slave's spirit is aided by that of the two old women in the task of guarding the money.

Motifs include E291 "Ghosts protect hidden treasure"; N576 "Ghosts prevent men from raising treasure"; and Thompson's D1815.1 "Knowledge of ghost language." Salt is frequently used in folk tradition as a means of protection against witches but its use as protection against ghosts is rare.

50. Collected July 15, 1961, by George Foss from Robert Shiflett in Browns Cove, Virginia. Shiflett was born in 1905 in "Shiflett Hollow" in Greene County, Virginia. His father, Erasmus, was a storekeeper in the area and the family moved to the mouth of Browns Cove in Albermarle County when Robert was a young child. Shiflett was known locally as "Raz's Robert" since he was the son of Erasmus. He was the brother-in-law of Mary Woods Shiflett, the widow of his oldest brother, who also contributed several narratives dealing with the supernatural to Foss. Robert died in 1979. The story may have been considered mainly as entertainment by Shiflett but it was also a bit of family history.

Motifs include E231 "Return from dead to reveal murder"; E235.2 "Ghost returns to demand proper burial"; E371.5* "Ghost of woman returns to reveal hidden treasure"; and E422.4.4 "Revenant in female dress."

51. Collected in 1940 by Lewis David Bandy from an unidentified white informant of Macon County, Tennessee. Although Bandy tells nothing more about the informant, there is no evidence in the text suggesting that it serves any function other than entertainment. Indeed, the structure of the text, with its almost formulaic opening and closing lines, is reminiscent of the *märchen* or fairy tale. Like many of the other texts in this volume this one has at least one narrative element more common to fairy tales than to legends. This feature is the "magic" fire which leaves Granny scared but unhurt.

Motifs included here are E291.2 "Form of treasure-guarding ghost"; E451.5 "Ghost laid when treasure is unearthed"; F473.1(ga) "Bed is thrown down and away from certain corner if it is set up there," which is very rare in folk tradition; N532 "Light indicates hidden treasure"; and Thompson's D1271 "Magic fire."

52. Collected by Lewis David Bandy from an unidentified white informant in Macon County, Tennessee, in 1940. Evidently the narrator believed the story was factual because he offers the concluding line, "It was all because of the hidden money." Motifs used are E371.4 "Ghost of man returns to point out hidden treasure," a narrative element widely known in England, Wales, Scotland, Ireland, Canada, and the United States and first reported by Scottish collector Robert Chambers in 1826; E402 "Mysterious ghostlike noises heard"; and E451.8 "Ghost laid when house it haunts is destroyed or changed." Although motif E402 is very common and widely known, the ghost who makes its presence known by the sound of falling rocks is relatively rare.

53. Collected by W.K. McNeil from Ella Fletcher of Onia, Arkansas, April 14, 1981. For more information about Mrs. Fletcher see the notes for her Text 28. Several widely traveled motifs appear in this text. They include E334.2 "Ghost haunts burial spot," and probably E371 "Return from dead to reveal hidden treasure" and E371.5* "Ghost of woman returns to reveal hidden treasure." The word "probably" is used because it is not altogether clear from the text whether the ghost is returning to reveal the treasure or to guard it. If the latter intent is involved then the motifs E291 "Ghosts protect hidden treasure" and E291.2.1 "Ghost in human form guards treasure" are relevant. The latter motif is well known in England, Wales, Canada, and the United States. Probably the best known instance of this motif is associated with a legend that the Scottish privateer and reputed pirate William Kidd (1645?-1701) buried a treasure on the Isles of Shoals sometime before his execution in 1701. According to the tradition that still-missing loot is guarded by a ghost. Comments made by Mrs. Fletcher throughout the interview suggest, though, that the ghostly woman was not guarding the money but rather, would have willingly told anyone who asked about it in the proper way that it was in her husband's grave. Also relevant here is E545.19.2 "Proper means of addressing ghost."

The idea of invoking the Lord's name in order to find out what a ghost wants is common in folk tradition, but the specific manner of address suggested here is uncommon. Generally, it is stated that the person must address the ghost in the name of the Holy Spirit and then ask its business three times. Some narratives say that the person must ask, "In the name of the Lord, why visitest thou me?" or "In the name of the Lord, why troublest thou me?" Yet others maintain that one must use the names in the Trinity in order to learn what the ghost wants. According to Mrs. Fletcher, merely having the Lord's name in the question asked of the ghost is the most important point.

Mrs. Fletcher found her father's reaction to the incident especially noteworthy: "He said he wasn't very scared. He said he sat down beside the road and thought he would rest awhile and he thought to himself, 'What was that woman doing behind that tree and how did she disappear?' I'll tell you, something like that would have scared me."

54. Collected in 1978 by Robert E. McNeill from Henry Dollar in Ashe County, North Carolina. Dollar was a thirty-nine year old white male with a high school education. Prior to being disabled by a gunshot wound he had been employed by a local chair company. The story related here was a personal experience of his grandfather that happened about the time of the First World War, i.e. 1916-1918. Thus, it was part of Dollar's family history, but it undoubtedly also functioned as entertainment. The Devil's Stairs is a local name for a spot in Ashe County, North Carolina that over the years has acquired a reputation as a place where macabre and mysterious things happen. Legends of supernatural happenings in the area postdate two deaths that occurred near there about 1910. The first, the accidental death of a black laborer by dynamite, happened about a year before the second, which was the murder of an unwanted baby by its mother. Many different types of ghostly sightings and encounters have taken place at the Devil's Stairs, including a number of reported versions of "The Vanishing Hitchiker" (see Texts 58 a, b, c, d, e and f). For more about these see McNeill's article, "Legends From the Devil's Stairs" in *North Carolina Folklore* 26:3 (November, 1978, pp. 149-156.

The main motif here is E332.3.1 "Ghost rides on horseback with rider" but E421.1 "Invisible ghosts" and E421.1.2(a) "Ghost scares horse" are also relevant.

55a, b and c These three texts are versions of one of the most popular legends found among Mexican-Americans, that of "La Llorona"—"The Weeping Woman." The first text was collected in 1965 in El Paso, Texas, by Cathy Skender from a boy raised in Ciudad Juarez, Chihuahua, Mexico. Skender gave no other data on the informant so it is hard to surmise how he used the legend or what meaning it had for him. Possibly he viewed it simply as entertainment and his text gives some indication of this attitude. Such phrases as "people reported" and "local people said" are the words of a reporter rather than a true believer but hardly conclusive proof of disbelief. Parents frequently employ the tale as a means of keeping children in check and away from certain places, and because this informant had known it from early childhood, possibly he first heard it used in such a way.

The second text was collected by William Campion from an unnamed seventy-two year old woman in El Paso, Texas. Since it is presented as a personal experience it obviously is viewed by the informant as something more than just an entertaining story. The third text was collected in 1963 in El Paso, Texas, by an unidentified collector from an unnamed informant. Related as an incident that happened to a close relative, this text also was regarded seriously by the informant. Possibly the narrative served as a localized temperance yarn since the implication is that the men only saw the ghost after a night of drinking.

Although "The Weeping Woman" is primarily associated with Mexican and Mexican-

American folk legendry, there is disagreement about its origin. In his article, "'La Llorona' and Related Themes," *Western Folklore* 19:3 (July, 1960), pp. 155-168, Bacil F. Kirtley maintains that "La Llorona" is largely of European origin and merely adopted in the New World. Most authorities, however, argue that it is a Mexican tale that has been around since Aztec times and is probably adapted from Aztec mythology. The Aztec goddess known either as Civacoatl, Chihuacohuatl or Tonantzin appeared dressed in white and carrying a cradle on her shoulders as if she were carrying a child. The goddess walked among the Aztec women and left the cradle alone; the women discovered that the cradle contained an arrowhead shaped like the Aztec sacrificial knife. During the night the goddess roamed through the cities screaming and crying until she disappeared in the waters of lakes or rivers. According to this thesis the myth later became merged with the story of a real tragedy, a case of infanticide that occurred during the sixteenth century. A peasant girl murdered her three children who were fathered out of wedlock by a noble-man. After dispatching the babies the mother went through the streets crying.

Whatever its source, "La Llorona" is known throughout the Southwest and as far away as the Phillippines. Wherever her adventures are recounted, the Weeping Woman is said to appear in many shapes and forms. She has a seductive figure and a horse face; she is dressed in black and has long shiny black hair, tin-like fingernails, and a skeleton's face; she is dressed in white, has long black hair, long fingernails, and a bat's face; often she has no face; sometimes she is a vampire. Meeting La Llorona is always a frightening experience and sometimes leads to tragic results. More often encounters produce such results as causing drunkards to reform their ways.

Of the three texts given here, the first one is somewhat unusual in that it contains no description of the ghost's dress and physical features. This legend also has the husband killing the children, thereby avoiding the usual motif of the woman returning as a ghost as punishment for the murder she committed. The second text is typical in that the ghost appears at midnight, the most popular time for the appearance of La Llorona. Although wailing is mentioned, nothing is said about the reason for the crying and, in fact, no association of the ghost with her dead children is made; these features are relatively uncommon but not rare. The third text is unusual only in that the ghost makes no sounds.

Motifs are E402.1.1.3 "Ghost cries and screams"; E422.4.3 "Ghost in white"; E547 "The dead wail"; and E587.5 "Ghosts walk at midnight."

56. Collected September 18, 1963, by George Foss from Lloyd Powell, Browns Cove, Virginia. For more information about Powell see the notes for Powell's Text 3. Apparently, the story given here was related primarily for entertainment. Despite his statement in the narrative, Powell was not fifty, but fifty-eight, at the time he related this tale to Foss. The only relevant motif is E425.1 "Female revenant."

57. Collected in 1968 by Bill Ferris from Gene Autrey, Leland, Mississippi. Autrey was ten years old at the time he contributed this text. Even though the narrative has a beginning similar to the "once upon a time" opening of *märchen* there is no evident reason to believe that Autrey didn't accept this as a factual story. There seems to be no motif number that parallels this tale.

58a, b, c, d, e and f These six texts are examples of what may well be the best known ghost legend in modern America, one that folklorists usually call "The Vanishing Hitch-hiker." The first text was reported by Billy Kyser, Fayetteville, Arkansas, in 1959 as recalled from a telling by his junior high coach, Pat Jackson, while on the way to a 1953 football game in Little Rock. Apparently, Jackson had a wealth of ghost stories to relate, for Kyser remembered that he generally told them to team members while they were traveling to games. This information makes it rather evident that this and similar tales were used as an entertaining way to pass the time while on the way to a game.

The second text was collected June 16, 1974, by Susan Jennings from her husband, Horace Jennings, in Trumann, Arkansas. The informant was a twenty-nine year old football coach who first heard the story in high school and recalled that it was mostly told on overnight hunting and fishing trips. In other words, the legend's main function to him was entertainment.

The third text was collected in 1962 by Judy Armstrong from Nancy Riley of Little Rock, Arkansas. Mrs. Riley had heard the story numerous times in and around Little Rock, primarily from older residents. It is unclear from information provided by the collector what Mrs. Riley's attitude toward the story is. Does she believe it is an account of an actual incident or is it just an entertaining story that happens to be well-known? Woodson is a community of five hundred located about twenty miles southeast of Little Rock.

The fourth text was collected in 1963 by Eugene Bourland from Elizabeth Kelly, a long-time librarian for the city of El Paso, Texas. Miss Kelly knew several other ghost stories, most of which she heard from a woman that she met while working at the library, that she told mainly for entertainment.

The fifth text was collected November 19, 1976 by Anna Farrier from Patty Faye Baker in Batesville, Arkansas. Unfortunately, the collector provided no additional information about the informant, but, because the narrative is offered as an account of a personal experience, one can assume that it serves a function other than just entertainment.

The sixth text was collected by Billy Kyser in 1959 from Freddy Akers in Fayettevile, Arkansas. Akers heard the story from Charles Abbott, a friend from his hometown of Blytheville, Arkansas, and previously heard an almost identical tale from his grandfather. Although the story was heard in Blytheville, the story is supposedly set just across the state line in Missouri. Apparently the story was seen by Akers primarily as entertainment.

Although the legend is well, and widely, known in the United States it probably did not originate here. It was, however, known in this country at least as early as the latter quarter of the nineteenth century but most likely was imported from Europe—or the story that may have been its prototype probably was. There is, however, also reason to propose an Asian origin for the narrative because a legend collected from Chinese immigrants in California contains many of the same motifs found in most early American versions. There is also a Korean version that was popular in the days before World War II. But, it seems most likely that "The Vanishing Hitchhiker" is an example of a narrative constantly readapted to changing times (to take newer technology into consideration, among other things) but ultimately derived from earlier European legends about eternally wandering ghosts such as "The Flying Dutchman."

Earlier texts of "The Vanishing Hitchhiker," of course, lacked the automobile, referring instead to travel by horseback or in horse-drawn vehicles. The automobile did not become a common feature until the early 1930s. Much older is the element of the hitchhiker's actual presence in the vehicle and her status as the ghost of a particular individual. Frequently, she leaves some object behind—a book, purse, suitcase, blanket, sweater, scarf, footprints, or water spots in the car. The driver often learns her identity at the hitchhiker's home by showing the object to her relatives, or describing her, giving the girl's name, or from a prominently displayed photograph of her that often shows her wearing the same clothing her ghost is dressed in. Sometimes she has borrowed clothing from the driver and it is found draped over her tombstone. Frequently she is picked up on a rainy night on a secluded road, but occasionally the pickup is made at a club or dance. Frequently the girl has been killed two, three, four, seven, or ten years ago, but rarely thirteen, the number most popularly associated with bad luck and which is used in a popular song based on the legend.

Over the years elements of various alien traditions have been blended into the story of "The Vanishing Hitchhiker." Besides "The Flying Dutchman," which has already been mentioned, characters and elements from Hawaiian traditions about the volcano goddess Pele, Mexican traditions about the spirit La Llorona (or "The Weeping Woman"), and from Mormon traditions about the Three Nephites, disciples of Christ who are said to appear to Mormons in times of need, have all become attached to some versions of "The Vanishing Hitchhiker."

The legend has also served as an inspiration for several movie shorts and television plots, the most notable of which is a thirty-minute drama used on the television series "The Twilight Zone." It also provided the story for "Bringing Mary Home," a song popularized by Billy Edd Wheeler and featured on his album *Goin' Town and Country* (Kapp KL-1479) and for "Laurie (Strange Things Happen)", written by Milton C. Addington and recorded by Memphis singer Dick Lipscomb, who records under the name Dickey Lee. The latter was one of 1965's biggest pop hits, reaching number fourteen on *Billboard's* Top 100 and remaining on the charts for thirteen weeks. Lee's recording was released on TCF Hall 102.

Of the six versions here, the first one, Pat Jackson's, is typical of modern Southern texts in that the pickup occurs on a night when the weather is dismal but is unusual in that the ghost remains silent. The feature of love at first sight is borrowed from romantic fiction although most texts reported to date the driver is very taken with the passenger's looks and personality. The latter feature, of course, can be dismissed here because the ghost is mute throughout, a fact that makes the idea of overwhelming love at first sight even more implausible. The other elements of Jackson's text are standard fare in modern versions of the legend.

Text 58b, by Horace Jennings, shows few deviations from other modern versions. It takes place on a dismal night on a road near a small community (Redfield is on the main route between Pine Bluff and Little Rock but is so small its population is not listed on most road atlases). That the driver learns of her identity from both parents rather than just the mother is a slightly different element in an otherwise conventional text.

The third text, by Nancy Riley, differs from most modern Southern versions in that no mention is made of the weather and the ghost talks to the driver after he arrives at her home. That she is on her way home for a holiday is also somewhat unusual, providing additional reason for the annual return. The unique feature of the fourth text is that the man who picks up the girl dies as a result of the encounter. A common motif in American folk tradition is death caused by meeting a ghost but it is rare in the modern tradition of "The Vanishing Hitchhiker."

The fifth version is distinctive, for it is one of the few reports of the legend that is related as a personal experience. Is it possible that the person merely presented a widely told tale in this format for dramatic effect? Or did she really have a supernatural experience? Since the collector supplied nothing more than the name, date, and place of collection it is impossible to do more than speculate on this matter. Another unique feature of this text is that the girl's death occurred only two months prior to the pickup, rather than the usual year or several years. Yet she apparently appears on "the night of her accident" which must mean that she is seen on the same night of the week her accident occurred.

In several respects the sixth text is the most unique of those presented here and may, in fact, represent an older form of the tradition since there is no actual hitchhiking; the meeting takes place as the man is walking by a graveyard. That the informant heard essentially the same narrative from his grandfather suggests that it is older. It shows some resemblance to a Chinese story collected from immigrants in California in which the ghost of a young girl walks with a young man along the road to her parents' home and then disappears. A significant difference is that the Chinese girl walks behind the man, thus he does not know of her disappearance until he turns around. This is, of course, exactly the way the driver learns of her disappearance in most automobile versions of "The Vanishing Hitchhiker." In the Chinese text the young man learns her identity from the girl's father. Also similar is Dickey Lee's song, "Laurie," in which the narrator meets the girl at a dance and walks her home, during the course of which she borrows his sweater. He later discovers she "died a year ago today" and finds his sweater "lyin' there upon her grave." In "Bringin' Mary Home" it is his coat that is draped over her tombstone but she had been picked up in a car on a "lonely road on a dark and stormy night."

Probably, besides sheer entertainment, "The Vanishing Hitchhiker" is offered by most narrators as a kind of exemplum concerning the perils involved in picking up hitchhikers. There may, of course, be many other possible explanations for the vast popularity of this particular legend. A book could be written on the subject and, in fact, one has, sort of. A portion of Jan Harold Brunvand's *The Vanishing Hitchhiker: American Urban Legends and Their Meanings* (New York: W. W. Norton & Company, Inc., 1981) deals with the legend. A discussion with numerous texts is found on pp. 24-26. Brunvand, and others, have labeled "The Vanishing Hitchhiker" an urban legend but it is no more urban than it is rural although, in most modern versions, an automobile, a symbol of urban technology, is prominently featured.

The motif is E332.3.3.1 "The Vanishing Hitchhiker."

59. Collected in 1973 by William E. Holloman from a Mrs. Holloman of Goldsboro, North Carolina, who is the collector's grandmother. Evidently this was not a story she had told often in recent years for it was recalled only with difficulty after the collector asked her for some local legends or ghost stories. She had the story from her grandmother and apparently used the narrative primarily for entertainment, telling it at social gatherings where ghost stories were frequently told. These stories generally followed games, corn-popping, taffy-pulling, or similar activities after which "guests would gather around the roaring open fire. They'd sit on the floor and tell ghost stories. After each one, someone would try to cap it and make it a little worse." After these sessions, Mrs. Holloman recalled that some people would act like they were afraid to go home.

The story Mrs. Holloman gave her grandson seems to have as its two main characters a George Deans (1831-1889) and a Rachel Vinson (1839-1857). At least there were two such actual people although only this narrative indicates there was any relationship between them. Actually, the connection is even more nebulous for it is a George Scott, not Deans, mentioned by Mrs. Holloman, but there is no George Scott that seems to fit the details of the story. The parting of the lovers is reminiscent of that in "Barbara Allen" and other Child ballads. They break up for some unknown reason—the informant suggests cold feet on the boy's part—and the girl soon dies from typhoid fever which, the narrator hints, may have been brought on by grief. For more on this legend see William E. Holloman, "The Ice-Cold Hand," *North Carolina Folklore* 22:1 (February, 1974), pp.3-8.

Motifs include E214 "Dead lover haunts faithless sweetheart"; E265.3 "Meeting ghost causes death"; and Thompson's F855 "Extraordinary image."

60. Collected in the 1930s by Claude Dunnagan from his grandfather who resided at Rockford in Surry County, North Carolina. Although the story about "Still Face" was told as an actual happening it seems likely its main function was entertainment. The narrator specifically emphasizes that it is "a story that's been told for years around Rockford" which, of course, is not irrefutable proof that the informant thought of it mainly as entertainment. Nevertheless, most Southern folk narrators do not use the word *story* for a narrative describing an incident they consider true and of serious import. Generally such a yarn is prefaced by some statement like, "Now this is no story, it really happened." The informant's attempts to explain "what really happened" to Still Face also indicate that he was at least skeptical about the supernatural aspects of the tale, as apparently were several other people in the community.

Motifs are E402 "Mysterious ghostlike noises heard"; J1769.2 "Dead man is thought to be alive" which is particularly popular in the South. Generally, this latter motif involves a story in which mourners are sitting up with a corpse that, due to some type of muscle contraction, sits up in the casket, causing the onlookers to think the dead man has come back to life. Also relevant here is Thompson's E261.2.1 "Coffin bursts; dead arises and pursues attendant."

61. Collected in 1961 by Jan Calhoon from Frank Allen of Crossett, Arkansas. Frank heard the story from a Negro he worked with who remembered the incident. There seems to be an air of superiority evident here, as though this is a story that "superstitious" people—meaning anyone that the narrator considers an inferior—believe, but one that he finds to be nothing more than an entertaining story. He emphasizes that "many other Negroes" believed the convicted man's tale about the two arms, possibly a deliberate choice of words suggesting that only Negroes believed the strange manner of revenge. Perhaps this is an erroneous interpretation of the narrator's views; his text may reflect nothing more than that the tale primarily circulated among Afro-Americans. All such speculation must remain guesswork because the collector provided no data with which one could draw any sound conclusions in this regard.

Motifs include E232.2 "Ghost returns to slay man who has injured it while living"; E234 "Ghost punishes injury received in life"; E422.1.11.3 "Ghost as hand or hands"; and Q285 "Cruelty punished."

62. Collected in 1960 by Jan Calhoon from Homer Davis of Urbana, Arkansas. Davis, who had lived in the area all his life, heard the story when he was a boy, which was approximately ten years before telling Calhoon the tale. The dilemma posed in the last line suggests that Davis thought of the story mainly as entertainment although he certainly believed events happened as described. Calhoon supplied the title "The Gusher of Blood" but there is no evidence that the narrator gave it any title. The motif here is E232.1 "Return from dead to slay murderer."

63. Collected in 1960 by Jan Calhoon from Maurice Lewis of Magnolia, Arkansas. Lewis had the story from Dick Dickson, also of Magnolia. Apparently, the story was just an entertaining piece of fiction to the narrator, who refers to it as "one story about the swamp." A related tale with a less violent ending is found in William Lynwood Montell, *Ghosts Along the Cumberland: Deathlore in the Kentucky Foothills* (Knoxville: The University of Tennessee Press, 1975), p. 123.

Motifs that apply here are D940 "Magic forests" and F990 "Inanimate object acts as is living." Calhoon gave this narrative the title "The Woods Are Alive," but evidently, the narrator supplied no title.

64. According to the WPA records this very literary sounding text is given exactly as told to J.C. Stutts of Cary, North Carolina by C.D. Creech of Moore County, North Carolina. If this text really contains Creech's exact words then it is certain that he had told this tale many times and had it all carefully rehearsed. His descriptions of "reedy, oak-shadowed banks" and "the raucous call of the katydids" have all the earmarks of a literary, rather than an oral tale—in any event, a narrative that has often been told. Although only the informant's name and place of residence are given it is obvious that he mainly thinks of the story as entertainment. A very dramatic manner with lots of dialogue and considerable lyrical description are used, exactly the sort of thing one might resort to when trying to present a suspenseful and interesting yarn of the supernatural. The General Greene referred to here is probably Nathanael Greene, the youngest of the generals elected by the Continental Congress. This is one of the very few reports of banshees, not only in Southern folk tradition but in that of the entire United States.

Motifs include Thompson's F491.5 "Will-o'-the-Wisp's revenge"; M301.6.1 "Banshees are portents of misfortune"; and Q467 "Punishment by drowning." The rain crow mentioned here is more commonly known as the cuckoo and, in folk tradition, is generally regarded as an omen of rain.

65. Collected April 19, 1981, by Aida Rogers from Julia Harmon Rogers, Cayce, South Carolina; Mrs. Rogers is the grandmother of the collector. Although she tells legendary narratives about the Devil's Track she has never seen the place. According to the collector the Devil's Track "is like a large footprint with a distinct toemark. It is remarkably symmetrical, and it is about ten inches long and five inches wide. The track itself is carved in the side of the rock, not the top, which makes it hard to spot. Also a rotten log has fallen down over the rock, covering it with leaves, dirt, and other debris. But the print is clearly visible." Possibly the narrative is told for entertainment but the collector feels that it also serves other purposes. She says, "I think it was told to inspire moral rectitude and to establish respect for the community. And after dwelling on the matter, I believe my grandmother once told me the legend in hopes that I would not lose my temper, and storm, rage, and fume like the little devil I used to be." Thus, like most folk narratives this legend is not always told for the same reasons; its purpose may change with each telling.

This etiological narrative has a suggestion of the elements of "The Devil at the Dance" but that portion of the present text has an entirely different result because the devil is not successful in his disguise. Motifs are A980 "Origin of particular places" and Thompson's A1617 "Origin of place-name." Although the concluding sentence of this text is incomplete, it is given here just as reported by the collector.

66. Reported by James Taylor Adams circa 1940 from his own memory. He had heard the story as a child from his mother and said he had heard it several times since in "slightly different versions." Adams (1892—1954) was a native of Letcher County, Kentucky, who spent twenty-five years as a coal miner in Wise County, Virginia. Leaving the mines in 1930 he spent the rest of his life as a printer and witch in Big Laurel, Virginia. He edited a quarterly magazine, *The Cumberland Empire*, that included sketches, short stories, poems, and songs descriptive of southern Appalachia. He also published a book, *Death in the Dark: A Collection of Factual Ballads of American Mine Disasters with Historical Notes (1941)*. For more information about Adams see Archie Green, *Only a Miner: Studies in Recorded Coal-Mining Songs* (Urbana, Illinois: University of Illinois Press, 1972), pp. 399-400. Thus, Adams was a person with a special interest in preserving various types of southern Appalachian folklore; for him it was much more than entertainment. His mother possibly believed in witchcraft although that is uncertain in this text.

Motifs include G265.4.1 "Witch causes death of animals" and G271.4 "Exorcism by use of sympathetic magic."

67. Collected February 4, 1941 by James Taylor Adams from Boyd J. Bolling, Flat Gap, Virginia. Boyd heard this story from his father and, as the text indicates, was inclined to believe the events described in the narrative were factual, primarily because of who told it, even though, apparently, he did not generally believe in witchcraft. Basically it seems that this narrative was told as local history and for entertainment.

Motifs include G265.8.3.1 "Witch bewitches gun" and G271.4.2(b) "Shooting picture or symbol of witch breaks spell (usually injuring or killing the witch)." The folk belief that if a witch or a member of the witch's family can borrow something from the family of the person who injured him then he will be cured is expressed here.

68. Collected July 15, 1961 by George Foss from Robert Shiflett, Browns Cove, Virginia. For further information about Shiflett see the notes to his Text 50. Shiflett regarded this story as part of local history, but mainly he found it an entertaining yarn. As some of his remarks indicate, Shiflett was not totally convinced that the marvelous events recounted in this legend didn't actually happen as described.

Motifs include D1700 "Magic powers"; D1721.1 "Magic power from devil" is implied; D1812.0.2.4 "Magic knowledge of witch (wizard)"; G200 "Witch"; G220.0.2 "Sex of witches"; G229 "Characteristics of witches: miscellaneous"; G249 "Habits of witches: miscellaneous"; G275.3 "Witch burned," which, despite popular opinion to the contrary, was a relatively rare way for a witch's life to end; G295 "Witch (usually male) does impossible deeds (usually with active aid of the devil)"; and Thompson's D1601.16.1 "Self-digging hoe," a motif that is primarily found in African and Asian societies.

69. Collected May 30, 1962, by George Foss from Robert Shiflett, Browns Cove, Virginia. For more information about Shiflett see the notes for his Text 50. Apparently, Shiflett told this story primarily for entertainment but also as evidence of the belief that local people once had in the power of witches. In Anglo-American folk tradition the violin or fiddle is often considered the devil's instrument, or box, and the legend given here corroborates the idea that musical ability really comes from the devil.

Motifs include D1751 "Magic passes from body to body"; G200 "Witch"; G224.10 "Witch power is transferred from one person to another"; and H1400 "Fear test." Although there are numerous texts and ordeals contained in various folktales and legends, the one reported here seems not to have previously been collected, which is why only the general motif is cited.

70. Collected July 15, 1961 by George Foss from Robert Shiflett, Browns Cove, Virginia. For more about Shiflett see the notes for his Text 50. Apparently, Shiflett regarded the narrative about George Herring and the others he related to Foss as local history but they were primarily valuable to him as entertainment. The degree of belief he had in the incidents described is evident from his statement, "That's taken with a grain of salt but most people in those days believed it."

Motifs include G200 "Witch"; G265.4 "Witch causes death or illness of animals"; and G275.12(b) "Witch as cat injured or killed by injury to cat." The borrowing mentioned in this text refers to the belief that if a witch is injured it will get well if it can borrow something from the person responsible for the injury.

71. Collected April 18,1963 by George Foss from Hilma Powell Yates, Browns Cove, Virginia. Yates was the sister of Lloyd Powell, another of Foss's informants, and, like him, was severely handicapped with a congenital degeneration of the eyes (their parents were first cousins). Born in 1903, Yates died in 1982. Evidently, she had little belief in the validity of the traditions about Jim Royal for she referred to them as "fairy tales"and "stuff." Still, she found them an entertaining aspect of local history.

Motifs include D600 "Miscellaneous transformation incidents"; G241.3 "Witch rides on horse"; and Thompson's D2188.2 "Person vanishes."

72. Collected in 1972 by Lovelace Cook from Carrie Patterson Shaver, an eighty-two year old black woman residing in Montgomery, Alabama. She definitely believed the incident described in her narrative really happened but there is also a possibility that this is a tale she sometimes told for entertainment. "Fennel leaves" refers to the perennial plant with yellow flowers that at one time was occasionally used for nature-made brooms.

Motifs include G241.2 "Witch rides on person" and G271.5(b) "Breaking spell by flogging witch."

73. Collected in 1981 by Gail Ogle from Burkett Casteel, a fifty-five year old white man living in Bristol, Virginia. Although Ogle provided no further information on the informant there is no reason to doubt that he believes this to be a factual report. True, the opening words "years ago" convey a similarity to the "once upon a time" opening of *märchen*, but that hardly constitutes evidence of lack of belief. Of course, Mr. Casteel may have been like some informants I have encountered who felt that witchcraft was practiced in times past but not in the past fifty years.

Motifs include G211.1.7 "Witch in form of cat"; G271.5(f) "Shooting or injuring in other fashion the form which the witch is using at the moment"; and G275.12(b) "Witch as cat injured or killed by injury to cat."

74. a, b, c, d and e. These five texts are versions of a very popular legend known as "La Hija Disobediente" (The Disobedient Daughter) or "The Devil at the Dance." The first text was collected April, 1965, in El Paso, Texas, by Janyth S. Tolson from Ernesto Chasco. The informant was twelve years old and a native of Mexico but an American citizen who received all of his formal education in Texas public schools. Although his family spoke Spanish they could neither read nor write the language; Chasco was comfortable with Spanish and had some difficulty with spoken English. Ernesto heard the story from his grandmother who believed it was a true story, and he apparently accepted it as an account of an actual incident, mainly because of his respect for his grandmother. As the last two sentences indicate, Chasco didn't accept every element of the story as factual. *"El Gato,"* the place where the disobedient daughter went, is Spanish for "The Cat." The phrase *"Eres pata de gallo"* means, "You are [have] a rooster foot."

Both the second and third texts were also collected in El Paso in April, 1965, by Janyth S. Tolson. The second one came from Alice Duran, a twelve year old native of El Paso, who heard the story from a babysitter who specialized in frightening the children with scary stories. The last sentence of this text reveals Duran's view of the story and its purpose. *"Pata de chivo"* means "foot of a goat." The third text was contributed by Roberto Guillen, a fourteen year old schoolboy, who said the story was about a true incident. *"Pata de gallo"* means "rooster foot."

The fourth text was collected in El Paso in 1967 by Pat Simons from Connie Herrera, an eighteen year old clerk for a local dry goods store. Herrera had the legend from her mother who said the incident happened about twenty years earlier, i.e. circa 1947, at Thomas Jefferson High School in El Paso. At the time Mrs. Herrera was a high school student at another school in El Paso. She heard the tale from her classmates who told it as fact. Mrs. Herrera said that people at the dance claimed the burning bush next to the girl was the devil, who had disguised himself as the "good-looking guy."

The fifth text was collected in 1968 by Mary V. Mellen from Mrs. Delia Zavala of El Paso. The informant was a married woman in her thirties and the mother of three small girls. She believed the incident described in her text really happened and, in fact, claimed to have seen the girl's face all covered with tiny scratches. She said the girl this happened to was the sister of a girlfriend.

Typically, "The Devil at the Dance" consists of a taboo or prohibition against dancing but a girl desires to attend anyway. The devil is at the dance, his presence is detected, he departs, and serious consequences result from his departure. That is the skeleton of the story, but there is considerable variation within each of these elements. The taboo exists for several reasons such as Good Friday, Holy Saturday, Lent; or simply a prohibition against dancing is imposed by the parents or grandparents. Sometimes the devil appears at the girl's house, is discovered and forced to leave. Sometimes she goes to the dance with the devil. In several texts it is a young man rather than a woman who goes to the dance. Sometimes the devil is already at the dance when the girl or boy arrives, and in other texts he arrives from out of nowhere amid noise or, in darkness, after the lights go out. In several texts he doesn't show up until after the dance is over. He appears most often either as a handsome, well-dressed young man, a musician, a young woman, a pig, a cat or a goat. His presence is usually detected by a physical feature, such as a tail, horns, unusual feet, claws, long fingernails, a protruding back that grows larger or by his manner of dancing. Generally a child, the devil's dancing partner, grandparents of the disobedient youth or some other older person, or a cowboy calls attention to the devil's presence. The devil departs in various ways, sometimes after the use of a religious charm. He often leaves in a cloud of smoke, amid a sulphurous smell, in an explosion, by flying out the window or up through the ceiling, by running out into the dark, turning into fire or simply disappearing into thin air.

The devil's departure often brings about some tragic or supernatural result. Sometimes the dancers find themselves at a remote spot or back at home; in some cases the dance hall itself moves from its place. Often the girl disappears with the devil, goes insane, is burned to death, or has her face scratched by the devil. On some occasions the devil scratches a girl's father or his image appears on the door and windows. In a few texts a musician receives a gift of food from the devil but, upon returning home, discovers that the food has turned into lizards.

The first text here is typical of most texts of the legend except that the priest's refusal to bury the girl in hallowed ground is unusual, especially since there is no indication that she did not die in a state of grace. The second text possibly was told to explain a unique scar or birthmark on the face of someone known by the person who related the legend to the informant. It is unusual from most versions of "The Devil at the Dance" because the victim ends up basically being a heroine, but one who has learned the proper lesson from her experience. There is nothing unusual about the third text, but the devil picking up the girl in a convertible, mentioned in the fourth text, is relatively uncommon. Generally such modern means of transportation are not used by the devil of this legend. The fifth text is somewhat unusual in having the girl married, a feature found in very few texts, presumably because married women are thought to be old enough that they are no longer under parental authority.

Motifs include G271.2 "Witch exorcised by use of religious ceremony, object or charm"; G303.3.1 "The devil in human form"; G303.3.1.2 "The devil as a well dressed gentleman"; G303.4.5.4 "Devil has cloven goat hoof"; G303.10.4.4 "Devils appears to girl who wants an escort for a dance"; and Thompson's C836 "Tabu: disobedience"; G303.3.3.5 "Devil in form of cock"; G303.3.3.1.6 "Devil in form of goat"; G303.4.5.9 "Devil has cock's feet"; G303.5.2 "Devil is dressed in green"; and G303.10.4.0.1 "Devil haunts dance halls."

75. Collected in Jonesboro, November 16, 1974, by Katherine Lemay from a nineteen year old college student from Forrest City, Arkansas, named Martha. Although Martha believes the story, it is also apparently used for entertainment, because she told it without prompting to several acquaintances at ghost-telling sessions. Possibly the supernatural incident serves as a means of acquiring status in her peer group. This is not a story so much as it is a description of some "strange" happenings involving a picture. Thompson's D1266.2 "Magic picture" is the closest relevant motif.

76. Collected by William E. Lightfoot, July 28,1977, from Precious Jackson in Sylvester, Georgia. Mrs. Jackson and her husband, Henry, are both physical and spiritual leaders in the black community of Sylvester. She is a retired schoolteacher, born about 1912, who believes she possesses God-given supernatural powers—such as bloodstopping and the ability to "talk" the fire out of a burn—that she tries to use wisely. Most of her stories concerning her power have happy endings, but in this text a tragedy results because she is not allowed to fully exercise her abilities. Thus, this and other stories about her abilities are told mainly as testimony to the validity of such supernatural powers as bloodstopping.

The relevant motifs here are D1504.1 "Charm stanches blood" and D2161.2.2 "Flow of blood magically stopped." "These words" referred to by Mrs. Jackson are a Bible verse used as a charm by many bloodstoppers.

77. Collected by William E. Lightfoot from Precious Jackson, July 28,1977, in Sylvester, Georgia. For more information about Mrs. Jackson see the notes for the preceding text. A discussion of dream-signs among Afro-Americans in the South is found in Newbell Niles Puckett, *Folk Beliefs of the Southern Negro* (Chapel Hill, North Carolina: The University of North Carolina Press, 1926), pp. 496-505, a book that has been reprinted by Dover Publications, Inc.

The relevant motif here is D1812.3.3 "Future revealed in dream," a frequent feature of fairy tales and legends.

78. Collected by William E. Lightfoot and Carl Fleischauer, August 4,1977, from Joe T. Fletcher, near Waterloo, Georgia. For more information about Fletcher see the notes for his Text 25. Both Mr. Fletcher and his father were bloodstoppers who practiced mainly on animals, especially calves that were newly castrated. The Fletchers would stop excessive bleeding merely by sticking a knife blade into the ground. As the concluding sentence in this text indicates, this memorate mainly serves as a testimonial to the validity of bloodstopping.

The relevant motif here is D2161.2.2 "Flow of blood magically stopped."

79. Collected by Henry Wacaster Perry in 1938 from Mart Rankins, a white resident of Carter County, Tennessee. Rankins, apparently, was a highly regarded local raconteur since he was called Uncle Mart, "Uncle" being a term common in Southern communities that has nothing to do with kinship but is instead reserved for respected older gentlemen. He also had a wealth of supernatural narratives, mostly about witches, and interrupted a series of witch tales to present this narrative about "a black thing." The speed with which the "thing" changed from two men into its black form hints that witchcraft is possibly involved. At the very least the tale is offered as a testimonial to the existence of things that can't be explained in usual ways.

Motifs are E530.1 "Ghost-like lights" and the following found only in Thompson: E422.2.4 "Revenant black"; K1821 "Disguise by changing bodily appearance"; and Z143 "Symbolic color: black." The slang term *batchin'* is commonly used by men, regardless of marital status, who are living alone and taking care of the housework. The term, of course, comes from the word *bachelor* and has been widely used since the late nineteenth century.

80. Collected in 1973 by Ralph C. Worthington, Jr. from a Mrs. Jim Barnhill of Pactolus, North Carolina. The informant was not eager to share this story with the collector and did so only after a great deal of persuasion by Worthington and coercion by her husband. Her reluctance was occasioned by her fear of being associated with "wild, outlandish" beliefs. She also saw herself as an old-fashioned person whose beliefs could become the butt of jokes by non-believers. She prefaced her story with the words, "Now this is not folklore because I saw this with my own eyes. This is true."

Motifs include Thompson's D1812.5.0.3 "Behavior of fire as omen" and F964 "Extraordinary behavior of fire."

81. Collected in 1939 by Robert Mason from his grandmother in Cannon County, Tennessee. She apparently had a large stock of legend material—another of her stories, a version of Type 1676B "Clothing caught in graveyard," appears in Text 27. Although the action takes place in and near a cemetery it is unlikely that any narrator presents this tale as anything other than a humorous story. Indeed, a Cave City, Arkansas informant frankly calls it a tall tale and most people who know this yarn would probably categorize it similarly.

This is a very widely known narrative that Thompson gives as Type 1791 "The Sexton Carries the Parson." Known throughout Scandinavia, the British Isles, Europe, India, the West Indies and, of course, the United States, this story is at least as old as the medieval *Thousand and One Nights* and appears in most medieval and Renaissance tale collections. The Mason text differs from most American versions in that instead of two boys dividing nuts or other articles in the cemetery, two sheep thieves perform this central action. This is exactly what generally happens in European versions of the tale and suggests that the Mason version was learned some years ago and has been little influenced by outside sources. A unique touch is provided by the addition of a man buried with hickory nuts placed under his head. Almost equally rare is the feature of the misunderstanding resulting from overhearing the thieves occurring twice. This expansion is typical of the entire text which is far more extensive than most reported versions. Such expansion and the considerable dialogue here are the marks of a skillful narrator.

There are, of course, many possible explanations for the widespread popularity of this tale but one is certainly its versatility. A teller can insert whatever he wants to be counted and various versions have the hickory nuts used here, or walnuts, fish, pawpaws, and sweet potatoes, but almost anything that is countable could be used. Undoubtedly the punch line in which one thief asks the other "Is he fat or lean?" or, in some versions, "One for you and one for me" or "I'll take the one over by the gate" is also partially responsible for its popularity. The absurd misunderstanding, no matter in what form, is a perennially popular feature of folk tales and it, and the surprise ending in which a severely handicapped person is not only able to run fast but actually outrun the able-bodied boys, also help the story's popularity.

Motifs here are X424 "The devil in the cemetery" and X143.1 "Lame man is taken on hunt on stretcher or in wheel chair. He beats the dogs home when they tree a 'hant' or when a bear gets after them."

82. Collected in 1968 by Bill Ferris from Wyndell Thomas, Leland, Mississippi. The informant was ten years old at the time and, as the son of James "Sonny Ford" Thomas, a noted blues singer, occupied a position of some prominence in the local Negro community. It is unclear whether Thomas believed this a factual account or not, but his calling it "a small story" suggests that he regarded it merely as entertainment. This is part of the cycle of Afro-American folk narratives involving John and his Old Marster. Richard Dorson said that this series of tales "provides the most engaging theme in American Negro lore." John is a trickster in the form of a plantation Negro in the antebellum South, a generic figure who enjoys a degree of favoritism and familiarity with the owner. For more examples of John and Old Marster see Richard M. Dorson, *American Negro Folktales* (Greenwich, Connecticut: Fawcett Publications, Inc., 1967), pp. 124-171 and Alan Dundes, *Mother Wit from the Laughing Barrel: Readings in the Interpretation of Afro-American Folklore* (Englewood Cliffs, New Jersey: Prentice-Hall, Inc., 1973), pp. 541-560.

There are no motif numbers in either Baughman or Thompson that parallel this tale but Type 990 "The Seemingly Dead Revives" does cover most of the details. It has previously been reported from the British Isles and the United States as well as most of Europe. Five versions titled "The Jewelry Thieves" appear in Montell's *Ghosts Along the Cumberland*, pp. 207-209. Montell thinks the legend originated in Europe and came to America with German immigrants. Almost every known text of this narrative identifies the item of jewelry as a ring. In most versions the thief cuts the ring off of the fingers of the presumed corpse, an act that causes her to awaken.

83. Collected by William E. Lightfoot from Lou Thacker, July 25,1973, at her home in Yorktown, Kentucky. Mrs. Thacker was born in 1927 and has always lived in the Big Sandy region of eastern Kentucky. She knows a large amount of supernatural lore, and her father was renowned locally as a blood-stopper. Mrs. Thacker told Lightfoot several accounts of bloodstopping, measuring, haunted houses, omens, and markings. Still, she is not a particularly skillful narrator as this text demonstrates. Her story has no dialogue and is presented in a rather uninterested manner, not unlike that which might be published by a newspaper reporter. There is a minimum of description with little more than the absolutely essential details being given. In short, this has all the earmarks of an oral narrative told by someone who is a passive legend teller. It seems that the only reason Mrs. Thacker remembers the story is because it was told by her father. Its function, then, is essentially the same as that served by a family history; it is, in fact, merely a piece of family history.

As Lightfoot comments, "This story is not a 'ghost story' as such, it does indicate an awareness of ghosts, and shows how belief in ghosts affects actual behavior." It seems likely, too, that the story is sometimes told as a humorous example of how belief in ghosts affects behavior. Two relevant motifs here are J1782.3 "House noises thought to be ghosts" and J1785 "Animals thought to be devils or ghosts." A similar story from Alabama appears in Browne, *"A Night With the Hants,"* pp. 161-162.

84. From Bert Vincent, *The Best Stories of Bert Vincent,* ed. Willard Yarbrough, (Knoxville, Tennessee, 1968), pp. 179-180. Vincent does not indicate the source of his story but, like most of the other stories in the book, it was taken from material sent in by readers of the Knoxville *News Sentinel,* most of whom come from Tennessee, Kentucky, Virginia, and North Carolina.

Perhaps the most popular motif here is one that is well known among both Afro-Americans and whites in the United States but is rare in other parts of the world. Baughman assigns this the number J1495.1 "Man runs from actual or from supposed ghost." It has been collected from Negro informants in New Jersey, South Carolina, and Florida, and from whites in New Jersey, Florida, Indiana, Wisconsin, Iowa, and Arkansas. That it is not even more widely reported is probably due to the fact that most American folklore collections have been focused on a relatively small portion of the country.

Other motifs here include E422.1.11.2 "Revenant as face or head"; J1495.4* "Man racing with ghost outruns rabbit" and three classified only in Thompson. These are D1610.5 "Speaking head" which is used in *Sir Gawain and the Green Knight,* in an Irish myth, and in Icelandic, Indian, and German narratives; D1641.7 "Severed head moves from place to place"; and E783 "Vital head" which refers to a head that retains life after being cut off. This latter motif is found, among other places, in stories from India, the West Indies, Spain, Ireland, and Iceland, although it usually occurs in *märchen* or fairly tales rather than in legends.

In most versions of this tale the cat is a revenent who talks to the man and later chases him, but here he merely provides a prelude to the real action. Since nothing is said about the informant it is difficult to determine what function this story serves for him. Judging solely on its submission to a newspaper column specializing in "interesting and unusual" stories it seems likely that the narrative is mainly used for entertainment.

85. Collected January 7, 1960, by Billy Kyser from Freddy Akers of Blytheville, Arkansas. Akers also contributed a version of "The Vanishing Hitchhiker" which appears in Text 58f. Akers heard the story given here in his hometown. A similar tale has a man falling in an open grave and, after several unsuccessful attempts to get out, decides to go ahead and sleep there. Then another man falls in the grave and while he is trying to get out the first man tells him there is no point, he can't get out. After hearing this the second man does succeed in getting out of the grave. Akers's text has an identical beginning but, of course, a different punch line from the other tale. There is no motif listed in either Baughman or Thompson that is relevant to the narrative given here.

Appendix 1
A Partial List of Folklore Archives Found in the South

Materials housed in these archives are generally available for use by qualified researchers, although there may be special conditions imposed on the use made of them. Anyone wishing to do research in these archives should make arrangements in advance of a visit.

ALABAMA

Archives of American Minority Cultures
P.O. Box S
University of Alabama
University, AL 35486

ARKANSAS

Regional Culture Center
Nana Farris, Director
Arkansas College
Batesville, AR 72501

Special Collections
University Library
University of Arkansas
Fayetteville, AR 72701

ASU Folklore Archive
Attn: Professor William Clements
Arkansas State University
State University, AR 72467

Folklore Archive
Attn: Professor Wayne Viitanen
University of Arkansas
Monticello, AR 71655

Ozark Folk Center
W.K. McNeil, Folklorist
Mountain View, AR 72560

FLORIDA

Florida Folklife Program
P.O. Box 265
White Springs, FL 32096

GEORGIA

Georgia Folklore Society Archives
Art Rosenbaum, Director
Electromedia Department
University of Georgia Library
Athens, GA 30602

Georgia Folklore Archives
Professor John A. Burrison, Director
Folklore Program
Georgia State University
University Plaza
Atlanta, GA 30303

Foxfire Fund Archive
Rabun Gap, GA 30568

KENTUCKY

Weatherford-Hammond Mountain
  Collection
Berea College Library
Berea, KY 40403

Western Kentucky Folklore, Folklife, and
  Oral History Archives
Helms-Cravens Library
Western Kentucky University
Bowling Green, KY 42101

Appalachian Collection
Ann G. Campbell, Curator
Department of Special Collections and
  Archives
Margaret I. King Library
University of Kentucky Libraries
Lexington, KY 40506

Appalachian Collection
Camden-Carroll Library
Morehead State University
Morehead, KY 40351

Appalachian Oral History Project
Appalachian Learning Laboratories
Alice Lloyd College
Pippa Passes, KY 41844

Robert Rennick Folklore Collection
Prestonburg Community College
University of Kentucky
Prestonburg, KY 41652

LOUISIANA

Archive of Acadian and Creole Folklore/
Oral History
Dupre Library
University of Southwestern Louisiana
Lafayette, LA 70504

MISSISSIPPI

Mississippi Folklore Society Archives
Committee
State of Mississippi
Department of Archives and History
P.O. Box 571
Jackson, MS 39205

Archives and Special Collections
University of Mississippi Library
University, MS 38677

NORTH CAROLINA

William L. Eury Appalachian Collection
Belk Library
Appalachian State University
Boone, NC 28607

North Carolina Folklore Archives
Curriculum in Folklore
University of North Carolina
Chapel Hill, NC 27514

Southern Historical Collection and Man-
uscripts Department
Wilson Library 024-A
University of North Carolina
Chapel Hill, NC 27514

Frank C. Brown Collection of North
Carolina Folklore
Manuscript Division
Duke University Library
Durham, NC 27706

East Carolina University Folklore Archive
Department of English
122 Austin Building
East Carolina University
Greenville, NC 27834

Bascom Lamar Lunsford Collection
Mars Hill College
Mars Hill, NC 28754

SOUTH CAROLINA

Department of Anthropology
Attn: Professor Robert McCarl
University of South Carolina
Columbia, SC 29208

TENNESSEE

Archives of Appalachia
The Sherrod Library
East Tennessee State University Library
Johnson City, TN 37614

Center for Southern Folklore Archives
1216 Peabody Avenue
P.O. Box 40105
Memphis, TN 38104

Archive of the Southern Folk Cultural
Revival Project
3390 Valeria Street
Nashville, TN 37210

Archives and Manuscripts Section
Tennessee State Library and Archives
403 Seventh Avenue North
Nashville, TN 37219

TEXAS

Sul Ross State University Archives
Wildenthal Library
Sul Ross State University
Alpine, TX 79830

University of Texas Folk Archive
Center for Intercultural Studies in Folk-
lore and Oral History
Social Work Building 306
University of Texas
Austin, TX 78712

North Texas State University Archives
A.M. Willis, Jr. Library
North Texas State University
Denton, TX 76203

Rio Grande Folklore Archive
Attn: Mark Glazer
Behavioral Sciences
Pan American University
Edinburgh, TX 78539

University of Texas at El Paso Folklore
    Archive
Attn: Professor John O. West
Department of English
University of Texas at El Paso
El Paso, TX 79968

Institute of Texan Cultures Library
P.O. Box 1226
San Antonio, TX 78294

VIRGINIA

Kevin Barry Perdue Archive of Tradi-
    tional Music *and*
The University of Virginia Folklore Ar-
    chive
Attn: Professor Charles L. Perdue, Jr.
Room 303
Brooks Hall
University of Virginia
Charlottesville, VA 22903

Virginia Folklore Society Archive *and*
The WPA Folklore and Folksong Collec-
    tions
Manuscripts Division
Alderman Library
University of Virginia
Charlottesville, VA 22903

Northern Virginia Folklife Center
Margaret R. Yocum, Director of Archive
George Mason University
4400 University Drive
Fairfax, VA 22030

Blue Ridge Heritage Library
Blue Ridge Institute
Ferrum College
Ferrum, VA 24088

Appendix 2
Directories

The following directories are also helpful in locating archival resources of Southern folklore.

Association for Recorded Sound Collections. *A Preliminary Directory of Sound Recordings Collections in the United States and Canada.* New York: New York Public Library, 1967.

Craig, Tracey Linton. *Directory of Historical Societies and Agencies in the United States and Canada.* Nashville: American Association for State and Local History, 1982.

Library of Congress. *National Union Catalog of Manuscript Collections.* Washington: Library of Congress, Catalog Distribution Services, Vols. 1-19, 1959-1981.

Shumway, Gary L. *Oral History in the United States: A Directory.* New York: Oral History Association, 1971.

Wasserman, Paul and Jean Morgan. *Ethnic Information Sources of the United States.* Detroit: Gale Research Co., 1983.

Wynar, Lubomyr R. and Lois Buttlar. *Guide to Ethnic Museums, Libraries, and Archives in the United States.* Kent, Ohio: Program for the Study of Ethnic Publications, School of Library Science, Kent State University, 1978.

Index of Southern Localities

The following entries refer to the text numbers utilized throughout the book. The locations referenced are mentioned either in the text itself or in its corresponding endnote. Additionally, some locations are referenced to stories contained in the general introduction; these are indicated by the number of the endnote which corresponds to that particular text. As with the main texts, the location may be mentioned in the text, the endnote, or both.